War Of Wrath And Ruin

FAE OF REWYTH BOOK 3

EMILY BLACKWOOD

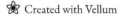

CHAPTER 1

Malachi

I saiah's blood-curdling screams ripped through the stone walls of the dungeons under the castle of Rewyth. He sat on the cold floor, chained to the damp wall behind him. His sun-yellow hair was hidden now, stained red along with most of his skin.

I lifted my arm and wiped the splattered blood off my face with my sleeve.

"You can scream all you want," I spat. He did. Isaiah screamed and screamed and screamed. After the weeks he had spent being tortured, I was surprised he still had a voice left. "Nobody will help you. Nobody is coming."

"You are a monster," he mumbled, although his words mostly blended together with his swollen lips and missing teeth.

I stepped forward with my small dagger. I had missed that dagger. Many warriors chose swords or large blades first, but there was something beautiful about the thin, sharp steel working its way through human skin inch by inch.

Much more painful, too.

I let the blade trail horizontally across the traitor's forehead as he thrashed against the chains. Blood fell into his eyes as he screamed once more and tried to flinch backward.

What a fool. Isaiah had nowhere to go.

A monster. I laughed quietly, pulling back and pacing the small cell. Being called a monster might have offended me once, lifetimes ago. Saints, I might have even started a fight over it. But now? A *monster*?

A wicked, feral piece of my soul flickered in delight. In recognition.

I was a monster, yes. Isaiah was *finally* seeing that. *Finally* understanding.

So many people *did not* understand.

So many people had *forgotten*.

They had forgotten who I was.

They forgot what I had done.

The fire of pain and chaos from my past ripped through my mind in the form of a distant memory. I saw all of it at once—all of the destruction. All of the evil.

The Prince of Shadows had been my identity for decades now, defining me before I even had a chance to speak in any room I entered.

Soldiers envied me. Children feared me. My father wielded me as his own personal weapon.

But I was no longer the Prince of Shadows.

Good.

I turned my back on Isaiah. What was left of him, at least.

King of Shadows.

Those who forgot what I would do to them would now

remember. The King of Shadows walked the halls of this castle.

And he would not arrive quietly.

CHAPTER 2
Jade

"Don't," Sadie whispered as I entered her cell. "If they catch you in here, they'll punish you for this."

I knelt on the ground next to her and emptied my pockets. A loaf of bread was the only thing I managed to sneak away this time, but it would be enough for her.

"I don't care what they do to me," I answered. "It's not fair that you're suffering. You had nothing to do with any of this."

Sadie shook her head. "It doesn't matter. I was close enough to Isaiah that I should have seen something. I should have caught on."

I shut her up by tearing a piece of the loaf and placing it in her boney hands. "Eat," I demanded. "You need to stay strong."

She obeyed.

We both pretended like we couldn't hear Isaiah's torturous screams somewhere in the depths of the dungeon. Sadie had been listening to it every single day for weeks now.

Even though he was a traitor, and even though I almost died because of him, I knew it hurt her.

She loved him.

And he betrayed her trust.

"Do you think things would have been different if Esther wasn't involved?" I asked her as she ate. "Do you think Isaiah still would have turned on me?"

Memories of my time with Isaiah flashed through my mind. He had been *kind* to me. He had saved me from the kraken in the river.

He asked me to leave Malachi for him. He swore I would be safe with him.

And then he conspired to kill me.

Sadie's eyes were focused on something that wasn't there. "I don't know," she whispered. "I don't think I know anything about him anymore. All this time I thought we were close, but it turns out he was a stranger."

A single tear left a watery trail in the dirt on her face.

"I'm going to get you out of here, Sadie. Just hang on a little longer."

She gave a half-smile, but her eyes never focused back on me. She had gone somewhere else. Somewhere deeper. Likely the same place she was forced to go to every day here in the dungeon to keep herself sane.

"I'll be back tomorrow if I can," I whispered as I stood up. "Just hang on."

My eyes had adjusted to the darkness of the dungeons. I had come down here as often as possible to check on Sadie, only bringing her food when I could spare some from the kitchen without being noticed.

Sadie didn't deserve this. I knew that.

But Malachi didn't see it that way. He saw them *all* as traitors. In his mind, Sadie was just as guilty as Isaiah.

I had to try talking sense into him.

My bare feet silently carried me through the dark tunnels of the underground. I had memorized the path by now. One long hallway and a left turn was all it took.

The temperature raised with every step I took toward the entrance of the dungeon.

I was close. Ten more seconds and I would–

"Enjoying the scenery, princess?" Malachi's voice echoed off the stone walls.

I froze, my bare feet halting to a stop.

"Yes," I responded without turning around. "The darkness can be quite beautiful."

A low growl rumbled the still air around me. "Sadie is down here for punishment. She doesn't deserve your company."

I spun around to face him, only to be greeted by a blood-soaked king.

That's who he was now, I supposed. *A blood-soaked king*.

Adrenaline pulsed through my veins.

"Sadie hardly deserves this. Torture Isaiah all you want, but Sadie did nothing to earn this fate."

Malachi clicked his tongue. "You know the rules, princess," he started. His voice had changed. It was colder now. Distant. "They almost got you killed. And you know just as well as anybody that I don't like people touching my things."

I stepped forward, now standing just inches from him in the darkness. "I'm alive, Malachi. And in case you have forgotten, Isaiah wasn't the only one who nearly killed me."

His breath hit my cheek as silence filled the tunnels around us.

I knew Malachi was in agony over what happened in Trithen. Not a day went by where I didn't think about it.

Malachi's blade to my throat haunted my dreams every night. I woke up screaming, drenched in sweat more nights than not.

He had made his choice then. He was protecting himself, I knew that. But I couldn't get myself to forget about the panic in my body. The hatred in his voice.

Malachi was a powerful fae creature, one of the most powerful fae in existence.

Only a fool would think otherwise. Even if that fool was his wife.

"Fine," I said eventually. "I'll leave Sadie alone." Malachi didn't say a word. "At least let me bring her a blanket or more water."

Malachi shook his head. His dark eyes reflected the tiny lantern light ahead of us. "You're too good, Jade Weyland. This world doesn't deserve you."

Weyland.

I didn't correct him, but hearing that name from his lips sent a chill down my spine.

"You don't like your name anymore?" he asked.

I shrugged. "I suppose I *am* still your wife, aren't I?"

Malachi stepped forward, a wicked grin spread across his face. "Until my dying breath, princess."

My stomach flipped, but I stepped back. "I should go," I muttered. "Adeline will be waiting for me."

"Wait," he said, grabbing my wrist. "Have dinner with me tonight."

7

My heart raced in my chest. I hadn't had dinner with him since the day after we had returned from Trithen, and even then, we barely spoke.

"Why?" I asked.

Malachi lifted a gentle finger and tucked a loose piece of hair behind my ear. His skin touched mine, just barely, and sent a spark of electricity through me. "Because I miss you," he whispered.

I would have ignored him...if it weren't for the way his voice cracked in hidden emotion.

I let a second pass between us before answering. "I'll think about it," I said to him.

His brows raised in surprise. "Okay," he stuttered. "Okay, great. I'll meet you in my dining room, then."

"And Mal?" I called to him as I walked toward the entrance of the dungeon. "Take a shower."

His soft laughter made me miss him, too. Even though I hated it.

I missed who Mal used to be. I couldn't deny that.

But that wasn't him. *This* was him. *This* was the new Mal, splattered in blood and torturing my old friends in the dungeons of his castle.

Yet he had touched me more than once and I hadn't flinched away.

Did he notice, too? Did he notice the way I allowed him to be close to me?

We hadn't had an exchange like that since before he held the knife to my throat in Trithen.

An exchange that didn't end in yelling or malice.

It was a start, I supposed.

Did I want this? I thought to myself. Did I *want* to rebuild my relationship with Malachi?

He was terrifying yet thrilling all at the same time. I couldn't keep my thoughts straight when he was near.

I did know one thing, though. No matter how much I said I didn't want to spend dinner with him...

I would be counting down the hours until I saw him again.

CHAPTER 3
Malachi

I showered three times to get every last drop of Isaiah's blood off my skin.

Normally, I would feel some sort of guilt or sorrow while I washed blood off of myself.

This time, though, I felt *satisfied*.

Isaiah and Esther needed to be punished.

We had let them live, which showed more than enough mercy. I should have killed them both for what they did. I should have ripped their heads off for hurting Jade.

But they were alive. Esther wouldn't shut up about how we needed her to save Jade's life, although she resisted telling us why. It was a ridiculous thought, considering she was the one who had put Jade's life in danger.

With Isaiah's help, of course.

I shook my head as the hot water ran down my back. How could I have been so blind? I should have seen it coming. I should have known Esther had an ulterior motive to help us.

She wanted me dead. She was going to kill me so that she could have unlimited access to Jade without *me* getting in the way.

That wouldn't be happening again.

Jade hated me right now. I knew that. I cursed to myself silently as I remembered how it felt to hold the blade to her throat. To pierce her delicate skin with my weapon.

She was terrified, yes. But I had no other option.

Did she not see that? Did she not see how *desperate* I was to save us both?

I stepped out of the shower and got dressed in my usual black attire, making sure to strap my sword tightly on my hip.

These days, I wasn't going anywhere without my weapon.

Not after my own power had failed me.

The wound in my shoulder from the poison arrow had healed over the last few days, but the memory of being so helpless remained stained in my mind.

Never again would I feel that weak. Never again would I feel so helpless.

Serefin waited to greet me outside my bedroom door. "Everything is ready," he announced as I stepped into the hall. "Just as we planned it."

I smiled. "Good. This is good. Thank you, Serefin." He nodded, but worry lingered in his eyes. "What?" I asked. "What is it?"

"I just really hope this is a good idea, bringing them here."

If it were anyone else questioning my judgment, I would have snapped. But Serefin's concerns were genuine. "Me too," was all I said. "Either way, they're safer here than they were in that poor excuse of a house."

"Agreed," he nodded. "That much is certain. They weren't happy about leaving, though. Be ready for a fight."

I laughed. "They're Jade's relatives. I expect nothing less. Anything noteworthy?"

Serefin shrugged. "The father is just as drunk as I remembered."

CHAPTER 4

Jade

I hadn't worn a dress since the fae festival back in Trithen. The black silk gown was loose enough to be comfortable, yet tight enough to expose most features. The time I had spent training was beginning to give shape and muscle to my lean body.

I looked stronger now.

I *was* stronger.

My black hair matched the dress, both coming together to create a dark shield between me and the rest of the world.

If only the shield were real.

Malachi requested dinner. I would allow at least that. Ignoring him had been the easy way out over the last few days.

But we were ignoring the inevitable. We were denying the truth.

I lifted my chin, looking at myself in the golden mirror ahead of me. The reflection before me was a far cry from the girl who had stepped foot in Rewyth the first time around. That girl had been naive and weak, even though she wanted everyone around her to believe she was strong.

I clenched my jaw and tilted my head to the side, taking in every healing bruise that covered my skin.

It was nothing compared to the wounds that ran deep. The secrets. The betrayals.

A whisper of anger tickled my stomach. I had been living off that deeply hidden emotion. Fury. Pain. Resentment.

It was the only thing I had. If I didn't feel those things, I might not have felt anything at all.

I lifted the hem of my gown and opened my bedroom door, all while ignoring the increasing pounding in my chest.

"Ready to be escorted to dinner, Lady Weyland?" Serefin spoke as soon as he saw me.

My chest tightened at the name, but I pulled my shoulders back and rolled my eyes. "How long have you been waiting out here, Serefin?" I asked.

He smiled, a familiar kindness returning to his dark eyes. I nearly smiled, too. "Just a few minutes. Malachi is waiting for you."

I turned in the castle's hallway and began walking in the direction of Malachi's dining room. Serefin followed closely behind me. "I don't need a bodyguard, you know."

"I know," he replied. "But I couldn't pass up the chance to finally see you. It's been a while."

"It has," I answered. I was glad I couldn't see Serefin's face. I knew the coldness in my words would have stung him, even if he tried to hide it.

"Look, Jade," he started, grabbing my arm from behind me and forcing me to stop walking. I glanced down at his hand on me. This was out of character for him. "I'm on your side, okay? We all are. I know you think we are the enemy right now, but we aren't."

I searched his face for malice but found nothing other than genuine care. Could I really trust him, though? The fae were the reason I was in this situation to begin with. If I had learned anything, it was that the fae were *not* to be trusted.

But Isaiah wasn't fae. He was human. *He* betrayed me.

Esther wasn't fae. She was a witch. *She* betrayed me.

The list of people I trusted grew smaller and smaller.

I swallowed the emotion that now stung my throat and looked Serefin straight in the eye. "You might truly believe that, but at the end of the day, I am a mere human in the pits of fae. If I have learned anything, it's that I am nothing more than a tool to be used in war. That won't change, Serefin. If I am the peacemaker, it can *never* change."

He opened his mouth to respond, but closed it again and nodded gently. "I am truly sorry, Jade. You don't deserve this life."

I placed my hand atop his. "Thank you, Serefin. The amount of people I can still trust seems to be dwindling."

He gave me a small smile and we both continued walking down the stone hallway.

"I know you believe his behavior is uncalled for," Serefin said in a low voice. I didn't have to ask who his words were about.

"I was wrong to expect anything else."

"Prince Malachi does what he does because he cares so deeply. I hope you can forgive him enough to see that one day."

I considered his words as we approached the dining room.

"King," I corrected.

"Excuse me?"

"You said *Prince* Malachi. I believe you meant *King* Malachi."

He shook his head softly and looked at the ground as we walked. "Yes," he breathed with a slight laugh. "*King* Malachi."

We didn't speak again until we had arrived at Malachi's dining room doors. "Thank you for accompanying me, Serefin," I said.

He smiled again as he pulled the large door open. "It was my pleasure."

Butterflies erupted through my stomach as I took the last few steps into the small dining room. I met Malachi's eyes instantly, they practically forced my attention. "Thank you, Serefin. We're okay in here," he said.

And the large door boomed shut behind me.

I froze where I stood, taking in Malachi's massive black wings that hung lazily over the dining room chair he relaxed in.

His massive, terrifying wings.

"Please," he started. "Take a seat."

His deep voice echoed off the dark walls. I waited a second longer before taking a seat across from him at the table.

"You look much cleaner," I observed, noting the lack of blood-splatter on his skin.

He smirked, but his eyes were locked on mine. *Always* locked on mine.

"I'm flattered that you noticed," he teased.

"Don't be," I retorted. "You'll be drenched in blood again in no time."

"Don't tempt me, princess," he growled as he leaned

forward an inch. "I tend to have too much fun when splattering blood is involved."

My breath hitched. This wasn't the Malachi I had grown to know. This wasn't the soft, protective man who hated killing.

"Don't call me princess."

"Why not?" he asked. "That is what you are, Jade. If not the–"

"Don't say it. I am not your queen. I never will be."

Malachi's brows furrowed as he stared at me. I would have given anything to know what was going through his mind. Did he want me to be his queen? Was he expecting that from me? I watched as his eyes glazed over, but he never broke eye contact.

Slowly, his emotionless mask reassembled.

He placed a hand over his chest. "You wound me."

I shook my head and gripped the armrests of my chair until my knuckles turned white. Malachi was trying to play me. "If you invited me here to antagonize me, then I should just go. There are better ways for me to spend my time, believe it or not."

He leaned back in his chair, finally cracking on the predator demeanor.

"Fine," he mumbled. "I invited you here for a nice meal. Let's eat."

I glanced around at the feast that had been prepared for us. Meats of all kinds, fruits I had never even seen before, and an assortment of fine wines littered the table.

My mouth watered just staring at it.

"This does not make me miss Fearford," I admitted.

Malachi huffed. "There's nothing to miss. We're home, and I don't plan on leaving anytime soon."

Home. I cringed internally at the word.

I may have considered Rewyth home. If it weren't for what had happened at Trithen...

"This isn't my home," I spat. "I'm only here to spare my own life from the Paragon. As soon as I can figure out how to survive this, I'll go back to my real home. Let's talk about that, shall we?"

I filled my plate with the tender meat as Malachi took a long breath. "Fine. Let's talk about it. Esther claims she knows something that will save your life, yet she reveals no further information. I've yet to decide if she can be trusted or not."

"She almost killed you."

"Yes."

"She would have used me as the peacemaker and left me to die as soon as she got what she wanted."

The crackling fire on the other side of the room grew louder. *Was it getting hotter in here?*

"Yes."

"What about you?" I asked.

Malachi's eyes met mine. I breathed slowly before he responded, "What about me?"

"Do you plan on killing me when you get what you want?"

He shook his head slowly, as if the thought alone was humorous to him.

"What I want?" he repeated, more to himself than to me. The fire crackled again, louder this time. "What I want is you,

Jade. How do I make you see that? How do I make you understand that I would give up any of this to be with you?"

My chest tightened, as if my heart was using every single ounce of being to not believe his words, even though every other piece of me wanted to.

One of Malachi's servants entered the room and set a fresh jar of water on the table. The small click of her shoes against the wooden floor was the only sound in the room as she walked away, closing the door behind her once more.

Of course I wanted to believe him. Of course I wanted it to be true.

But that was a fairytale.

"Well," I coughed, changing the conversation. "We know I have magic now. I suppose I can't keep denying that I am the peacemaker."

"No," he agreed. "We can't. You used your power when you were desperate. We'll have to work on your control. It will grow stronger every day that we ignore it."

"And what exactly am I supposed to do with it? Just walk around and save the world?"

Malachi smiled wickedly. "Unfortunately for us, we're never that lucky."

Luck. Such bullshit.

"You're telling me you haven't talked to your mother since we've arrived back here? Too busy with Isaiah?"

"Isaiah deserves to die. Let's not get into this again, Jade. Esther will be handled when the time is right."

My name rolling off his lips evoked an emotion I had been burying deep down.

"Then kill him and be done with it," I spat. "He was

looking out for himself and he chose the wrong side. Where does torturing him get you?"

Malachi leaned back, once again lazily draped over the chair. He picked up his porcelain cup and took a sip of liquid before setting it down again. The cup clinked against the saucer before he replied. "Let me ask you something, princess. What do you suppose the others think when they hear Isaiah's screams echoing through the dungeons? What do you suppose they would have thought if I had shown him mercy and killed him?"

I clenched my jaw and stayed silent. A bead of sweat began to form on the back of my neck.

"I am the new King of Rewyth. People will challenge me. People will try to undermine me. People will threaten my rule, Jade. They will threaten the people I care about. They will threaten you."

"So you torture Isaiah to send a message? A warning?"

"You almost died because of him. Why do you care? Why are you protecting him?" His mask cracked as his temper flared. I saw the wild emotion growing behind his eyes.

"He's a human being," I pleaded.

"He is a traitor! He is a snake!"

I bit my tongue. Isaiah wasn't the only snake.

"And what about the others?" I asked. "What of Sadie? Of Esther?"

"I don't know yet. But I do know one thing. Anyone who threatens you will die, Jade Weyland. They will die by my hand, and it will not be swift. If Isaiah must be the messenger for that, then so be it."

I set my fork down and leaned back, matching his body language. "I can fight my own battles, you know."

Enlightenment flickered across his features. "After what happened with your power back in Trithen, I think it's safe to say that you're going to become one terrifying woman."

"*Become* one?"

Malachi gave me a teasing wink. "All in due time."

I rolled my eyes again and continued eating. After a few minutes of silence in the room, Malachi leaned forward and placed both elbows on the table. "You disintegrated a cage made of bone, Jade. That deadling melted to ash. I should be lucky I wasn't roasted with it."

I shook my head. "It all happened so fast, I don't even know what I did to make that happen."

"You were desperate. Your power saved you."

"Is that what your power does?" I asked, genuinely curious. "Saves you when you're desperate?"

Malachi's gaze shifted into the space behind me as he thought. "It started off that way, yes," he answered. "But over the decades, the darkness has become a part of me. It's right here with me every second of the day. It acts on its own, but never without my permission. It's second nature."

I nodded, wanting him to continue.

"It took a long time to get to this point, though," he said. "There were times when I lost control. There were times when my power became a burden instead of a tool. It was destructive and brutal, but I was the one paying the price."

"What price?" I asked.

His eyes snapped back to mine. "Sanity."

Something dark within me stirred. "You think that will happen to me?" I asked in a whisper.

Malachi's jaw tightened. He rested his chin on his fist as

he stared at me. "Never," he answered. "I won't let that happen."

My first instinct was to defend myself. I didn't need Mal watching over me. I could take care of my power on my own.

But I knew, deep down, that I needed him. I needed his help to control my power.

"Okay," was all I managed to say.

The doors to the dining room suddenly ripped open, causing me to jump in my seat.

Malachi tensed immediately. "What is it?" he asked the guard who entered.

"There's a problem in the castle's dining hall, King Malachi," he said. "Your presence is requested."

Malachi tossed his head back and exhaled a long, exhausted breath. I observed him closely, noticing the way he rubbed his hands across his face.

Malachi would make a great king. I never doubted that. But I also knew that deep down, the pressure would get to him.

"Fine," Malachi answered. "I'll be there in a moment. Leave us."

The guard nodded and left the room, leaving Mal and I alone once more.

"Duty calls," I mumbled.

"Not yet," he said. "I have something to show you."

He stood up and walked toward the rear entrance of the dining room. When I didn't follow, he stopped in his tracks. "Are you coming?" he asked.

"Why should I?"

"Trust me," he pushed. "You're going to want to see this."

I debated my options. I could sit there being stubborn,

being difficult in any way possible and refusing to cooperate. Or, I could follow him, which would undoubtedly be seen as a win in his eyes.

I had to admit, though, I *was* curious.

"Fine," I said, standing from my chair. "But if this is a trick, I'm taking my power out on you next time."

Malachi laughed quietly. "I'd expect nothing less."

I followed him through the door into a dark hallway. "What is this?" I asked.

"These are the old servant quarters. We haven't used them in ages, but they're still here."

I instinctively reached forward to grab Malachi's hand in the darkness, but pulled back once I realized what I was doing.

"Dark, secret, abandoned tunnels in the fae castle. Sure. Not creepy at all," I mumbled.

"We're almost there," he ushered. "It's just right up...yes. In here." He twisted the doorknob on an old, wooden door and pushed it open. "After you."

I stepped forward and ducked through the dark doorway. The air was much warmer inside of the room, and my eyes quickly adjusted to a few lanterns of light.

"Jade?" a voice I recognized squeaked from the back of the room.

And then my eyes found Tessa.

"Saints," I whispered. "Tessa."

I wanted to run to her and crush her in my arms, but after our last interaction, I was hesitant.

Tessa had been terrified of Malachi. Terrified of *me*.

But now, that seemed like a lifetime ago. Things could change. Feelings could change.

Tessa didn't say anything, but her eyes darted between me and Malachi, who still stood behind me. That's when I noticed my father huddled in the corner of the room.

"You brought them here?" I asked Malachi without looking at him.

"They aren't safe at home. I figured you would–"

"Thank you," I interrupted. "Thank you for bringing them."

I couldn't see Malachi, but I felt his breath as he exhaled slowly, just inches behind me in the darkness. "I'll leave you all to get reacquainted, then," he said.

And then the door was shutting behind me. A cool breeze tickled my skin where he had just been standing.

"You're still alive," Tessa whispered. "I–I thought you might be dead."

I took a deep, calming breath and stepped forward, closer to my sister. "I'm still alive," I responded, trying to be as gentle as possible.

"Good," she replied. She folded her hands in front of her and glanced down at her feet. "I...I wouldn't want you to die."

I shouldn't have felt relieved by that statement, but I did. "That's good," was all I could manage to say. *Really, Jade?*

My father snored loudly from the corner. "He's been sleeping?"

"Pretty much since we arrived here. Although he spent the first few hours yelling about being kidnapped."

"Kidnapped?"

Tessa took a long breath and stepped forward, letting the dim light of the lantern hit her face. She looked older. Harsher.

Not the innocent, naive girl I had left back home.

"It was the middle of the night. They tried to tell us they were helping and that they were taking us to you, but he wouldn't listen."

I looked over at my father. The man had become a stranger to me. He looked much older now, even though we had only been apart for a short time. Deep wrinkles lined his forehead and his cheeks had sunken into his face, causing his cheekbones to jut out much sharper than they had before.

He looked much older than he was. He looked...*sad.*

I cleared my throat and turned my attention back to Tessa. "I can't say I'm surprised. He's never exactly been a great listener."

A long moment of silence passed between us. Tessa looked at me, drawing her eyes over each of my features. It was as if she were really seeing me for the first time.

"We missed you, you know," she said. "When you came to see us back home we...we were surprised. And the fae prince was..."

"I know," I interrupted, recalling the details of Malachi pinning our father to the ground outside our front door. "I didn't mean for anything like that to happen. I didn't mean to scare you."

Tessa broke our eye contact and glanced at the floor once more. "It was unexpected. That's all. We didn't even know if you were alive."

"I know," I said again, softer this time. I wanted to reach my hand out and grab hers, but I resisted. I'd been doing a lot of that lately, it seemed. "Malachi...he's not as bad as he seems. I promise you. He's kept me safe this whole time. He'll do the same to you."

Tessa nodded slowly. "You're different now," she stated. "You seem like you've changed."

The words pierced me like a dagger to the chest. "I *am* different," I whispered. I fought to keep my voice steady against the wave of emotions that rushed forward. I had changed. Not because I wanted to, though. No. I changed because I *had* to. Because I *had* to survive. I changed for *us*. For *Tessa*.

For myself.

"A lot has happened since I married Malachi," I said. I chose my words carefully. "I've come so close to death I should feel lucky for even standing here right now."

Tessa smiled gently, but it didn't reach her eyes. "Do you?" she asked.

"Do I what?"

"Do you feel lucky to be alive?"

The air rushed from my lungs. My life had been the furthest thing from *lucky*. I had been bartered away to the fae prince, who now tortured humans in the dungeons of his own castle. I had nearly been killed by assassins, a tiger, a kraken, multiple deadlings, and *my own husband*. The only reason I had for surviving at the beginning of all this was Tessa. I wanted to make sure she lived a long, happy life.

But Tessa grew up. She survived without me. She didn't need me anymore. She was no longer the ignorant girl I once viewed her as.

Without Tessa forcing me to keep fighting, to keep living, what did I have left?

Malachi?

Was I *supposed* to feel lucky? Was any of this supposed to make me feel lucky for not being dead?

I couldn't tell her that. I couldn't tell her any of it. She wouldn't understand what it was like to feel this endless pit of numbness. This welcoming emptiness.

"I think I do feel lucky," I lied. I lifted my chin and rolled my shoulders back. "Rewyth is a great home. I think soon enough, you'll be feeling pretty lucky, too."

Her expression changed entirely. "We're staying here?" she asked. I noted the small trace of panic that laced her words. "Forever?"

"It's not safe for you back home right now," I stated. "There are people who want me. They would find you and use you to get what they want."

"Who? The fae?"

My father began to stir in the corner. I wanted to explain, I really did. I wanted to tell Tessa everything that had happened so she would understand. So she would trust me again.

I saw the hesitation in her eyes. I saw the doubt.

But confronting my father right now was not in my best interest.

"I'll tell you everything," I said. "I'll come find you later and I'll explain it all." My father moved again and began mumbling words incoherently. "I just...I have to go."

I backed up, stepping closer and closer to the door I had entered from. "No," Tessa argued, stepping forward after me. "Don't leave."

"I promise I'll come for you, Tessa. I promise."

My father said something again, finally beginning to understand where he was and what was going on, as I slipped into the dark hallway and sealed the large door behind me.

I didn't look back.

CHAPTER 5
Malachi

"**G**et up," I barked.

Eli draped himself over a bench in the gardens of the castle, passed out, with an empty bottle lying next to him.

When he didn't respond to my words, I kicked his foot. Not hard, just enough to wake him up.

His eyes blinked a few times before opening completely. And as soon as he saw who stood before him, he groaned and tossed his head back.

"I said get up," I repeated.

"What for?" he replied. "Are we at war so soon?"

I took a deep breath. I felt horribly for Eli, I did. He had lost his twin. His other half.

There were few memories I had of Eli that Fynn wasn't also involved in. And now, Fynn was dead. And Eli had nothing.

But I couldn't watch him sit around the castle and rot any longer. "Adonis and Lucien are on their way. We have to talk."

Eli laughed. Cold and bitter. "Apologies, brother. But I don't think I'm really in the mood to chat."

I looked to the sky, willing any sort of patience from the Saints to save me from biting his head off. "I know you're in pain, Eli," I said, "but you can't keep doing shit like this. We have a kingdom to run here, and I need your help."

This seemed to amuse Eli even further.

"Rise and shine, brother," Lucien's voice carried into the garden as he and Adonis approached. "The King is requesting your assistance."

Lucien bowed dramatically to make his point.

I rolled my eyes.

Adonis walked up slowly behind Lucien. "You look good, brother," Adonis said to me. I hadn't seen him since our return to Rewyth. I wasn't avoiding any of them, but I wasn't exactly going out of my way to speak with them, either.

Until today.

"We need to talk," I repeated to my other brothers. "Esther is rotting in that dungeon. If we don't make a plan soon..."

I didn't have to finish the sentence. Adonis and Lucien knew the seriousness of the situation. Esther was a powerful witch, but she was rotting away down there. If what she said was true, we needed her.

But how could we trust her?

"You want us to give you advice?" Lucien asked. "Aren't things supposed to be the other way around?"

"You were all there. You were sworn to her blood oath. You know more about her character than I do."

"What do you want us to say?" Adonis chimed in. "The woman is a witch. She's selfish and greedy. Jade is the peacemaker, and Esther wants to use her power for her own benefit."

I considered his words. He stated nothing but facts, but he still didn't offer a way out. "If we kill Esther," I started, distancing myself from the words as I spoke them, "we'll have no idea what's coming. She claims she knows a way to break this prophecy. Jade won't have to die."

"Have you spoken to her about it?" Adonis asked. "How can you know she's telling the truth? What if she's making this all up?"

I took a long breath. "I can't know," I said. "Which is why I haven't spoken to her since we left Trithen."

"You're kidding, right?" Eli chimed in from the garden bench. He sat up now, somewhat paying attention to the conversation happening around him. "She's the reason Fynn is dead. She deserves to die."

Silence filled the air.

He wasn't wrong. If Esther hadn't worked with Isaiah and Seth to try and kill me, Fynn would still be alive.

But that was the past. If I spent a single minute thinking about things like that, my entire world would collapse around me.

"We can't kill her if she's useful to us," I said, trying yet failing to soften my words. "She's valuable."

"For what?" Eli asked. "To save your human wife? No offense, brother, but I don't really give a shit if Jade lives or dies. Why should any of us care? What is she to us?"

A low whistle escaped Lucien, but my temper was already on fire. If Eli hadn't looked so pathetic already, I would have pummeled him to the ground. Instead, I lifted my chin and clasped my hands behind my back.

"I know you're going through a hard time right now, Eli, but if you say that type of shit again, you'll pay. Understand?"

Eli stared at me with wide eyes but said nothing.

I continued. "This prophecy is equally as important to us as it is to the witches. As it is to the Paragon. If Jade fulfills this prophecy and we are the ones to help her, the fae will be the ones to inherit the power. How would you like to have magic unmatched to any in the world, Eli?" I asked. "How would it feel to be so powerful, not a single enemy could take you down?"

Now I had their attention.

"If the Paragon comes for Jade, they will be the ones to fulfill the prophecy. They will be the ones to inherit the power. And then we will be nothing. We won't stand a chance against them."

"If they come for Jade," Lucien interrupted, "there's not much we can do to stop them."

I nodded. The Paragon was powerful. That much was no secret.

But so was I.

I tried to recall each of the special powers they possessed. If what I remembered was still true, they had a strong warlock who had no limit on controlling the elements. He did not tire. He did not pay any price.

I also remembered a man, a fae, who could freeze a person with just a stare. One look, and his opponent wasn't able to move a single muscle.

There were others, too. Fae and witches both with powers unheard of in other kingdoms.

Much like myself.

They would have strength in numbers, but nobody was

certain they would even appear here in Rewyth. That was simply another piece of information Esther had given us, likely spun deeply in her unending web of lies.

"If they come for her, I'll kill them. Every single one of them."

"Can you do that?" Adonis asked. "The Paragon is smart. They won't come alone. They won't come unarmed. They'll have a plan."

"They will," I said. "But so will we."

"And what if they don't even know of Jade yet? What if Esther has made this entire thing up for her own benefit?"

"Then we'll kill her, too," I said. Agitation laced each word, but I couldn't bring myself to care. I was now the King of Rewyth, the most powerful fae kingdom in the lands. Nobody would question our power. If anyone tried to take what we owned, what I owned, they would pay with their lives.

The more I had to explain that to people, the more annoyed I became.

"Eli," I said, bringing my attention back to my drunk brother. "I need you to talk to her. Go befriend her. Find out what she knows."

This caught his attention. "Me?" he asked. "Why me? Why not Adonis?"

"She'll see Adonis or Lucien as a threat. She'll see you as someone who is hurting and wants answers."

Pain flashed through his features. I continued. "She's in the dungeons, but don't speak to anyone else. Especially Isaiah."

Lucien huffed.

"Something to say?" I asked him.

He shook his head. "Nothing," he started. "It's just that you keep torturing the human and you haven't laid a finger on the witch."

I knew this was coming. "It isn't her time yet," I said. "She'll get what she deserves."

"And will that be before or after we go to war with the Paragon?" he asked.

My power pulsed through my body, waving with each of my emotions that I seemed to be having less and less control over. "Enough of this," I barked. "I know we are brothers, but I am the King of Rewyth. My word is final, now. I got us into this mess, and I'll get us out. Nobody touches Esther without my say. Nobody interferes with Isaiah without my say. Understood?"

"And Seth?" Lucien asked. "We're going to let the King of Trithen live after what he's done?"

A wicked grin spread across my face. "His time will come, too. We have to be patient."

"Fine," he said. "But I do know one thing, brother. If others see us as weak, they will attack. The Paragon, Trithen, whomever else. Torturing the human in the dungeon does not show strength, brother. It shows hesitation. It shows weakness."

I didn't say a word.

"Just something to think about," he said as he walked past me, clapping me on the shoulder.

"Where are you going?" I asked after him.

Lucien didn't turn around as he answered, "I'm going to go live my life while I still can, brother," he said. "War is coming. I don't know when, but I can feel it. And I have a feeling Fynn was not the last of us to die."

Isaiah didn't react as I stepped into his cell. He had stopped reacting after the first few days—once he realized protesting wasn't going to help him.

Most of the blood on his body had dried. I stepped forward and unscrewed my flask of water.

"Open your mouth," I demanded. He twitched lightly, but didn't move any more.

I grabbed the back of his head and pulled his hair before drizzling the liquid over his face. If he didn't want to drink, that was fine by me.

After a few seconds, he began licking his lips. I drizzled a small amount more before letting go of his head and screwing the top of the flask back on. "Are you ready to talk?" I asked.

Isaiah only shook his head.

"Tell me what Esther really wants," I demanded. "Tell me why you turned on Jade."

The smallest hint of a smile betrayed him.

He opened his mouth to speak, making a couple of attempts to use his voice before finally saying, "She would have been safer with me."

A laugh escaped me. Isaiah must have been more delusional than I gave him credit for. "How, exactly? Considering you were the one who conspired to kill her, I have a hard time understanding how you could have kept her safe."

Isaiah tried to look at me, barely able to open his swollen eyes. "I asked her to leave you, you know. I begged her to leave you and come with me back to Fearford." Every muscle in my body stiffened. "She refused, of course. Jade surprised me— she really did. She wasn't the…" A coughing fit interrupted him. "She wasn't the helpless human girl enslaved to you. She wanted to be with you."

Anger flooded my senses. Dripping water in the distance was the only sound in the cell. Why was he telling me this? Why now?

"She knows I will protect her," I admitted. "Something you could have never done."

Isaiah's breath became labored as he slowly struggled against the heavy chains. "You will be the end of her. You will try to protect her, but you will fail."

"You know nothing," I hissed. "You are a traitor and a liar. Why should I trust anything you say?"

"I never wanted to hurt Jade. I only wanted her to see the truth." I clenched my jaw as I waited for him to say more. Isaiah's eyelids began drooping once again, "We can all see it," he whispered. His voice was barely audible in the dungeons as he continued, "We can all see that you will be Jade's downfall."

His bloodied head sagged against his chest.

I threw the flask into his lap and stormed out of the tunnels, ignoring the angry shadows that lapped at my dwindling consciousness.

CHAPTER 6

Malachi

Seconds after I dressed in clean clothes, Jade marched into my bedroom without a single knock.

And she looked pissed.

"Were you going to tell me you practically kidnapped my family and dragged them here?"

"What?" I asked, sitting up in my tall bed. "I thought you would enjoy the surprise!"

"You can't make decisions about my family without me," she demanded. Fury swarmed her dark eyes. I loved the wildness in Jade. I always had. She was a strong, powerful woman and she was as complicated as anyone. "I should have had a say in the matter!"

"You're not happy about it?" I asked, tip-toeing with every word.

Jade shook her head, running her hands through her long, black hair. "No, I–It's fine. I just would have liked some sort of warning. I could have prepared, I could have–"

"Could have what? Come up with a huge lie as to what exactly has been going on?"

She stopped pacing and met my gaze. "I'm going to tell them the truth. Tessa deserves to know."

I admired her honesty, I really did. But telling her younger sister the truth about the prophecy wasn't going to help anything.

"Is she still frightened?" I asked, keeping my voice low.

Jade crossed her arms. "Of you? Yes."

I deserved that. "And what about you?"

I watched as Jade's chest rose and fell slowly with a long breath of air. "It's not me she's afraid of," Jade said. Her voice shook slightly, but she continued anyway. "It's...it's the things I've done."

I waited a few seconds before asking, "And what have you done that is so terrible?"

Jade looked at me as if I had said something ridiculous, but the fact that she thought she did anything wrong was ridiculous to me. Jade was a victim. She was dragged here and thrown into this world with no say. All she wanted to do was protect her sister.

And now she was the peacemaker with a massive target on her back.

Yet her only family made her feel *guilty* for surviving?

I wasn't going to sit around and listen to this.

"I've done so many terrible things," Jade said. Her eyes were wandering around my bedroom, but I knew she was lost in thought.

Lost in the demons of memory.

"You did what you had to do to survive," I reminded her. "You have nothing to be sorry for, Jade. You have nothing to apologize for. Especially not to your family. You did this for them."

"Tessa won't understand," she continued. "Humans and fae...I shouldn't have been...I mean..."

"She expects you to hate us all," I finished for her.

"Yes," Jade admitted. "She does."

I stood from my bed, very aware of the fact that the thin trousers were the only thing I wore. Jade's eyes didn't leave mine.

Although I noticed the way she stiffened when I stepped toward her.

"Are you saying you *don't* hate us all?" I pushed.

Jade swallowed once. "I didn't say that."

"No," I said, taking another step forward. I half-expected Jade to back up, but she didn't.

Stubborn girl.

"You said Tessa expected you to hate us all. And somehow that's a problem." It was risky, but I reached out and picked up a piece of her shiny hair, letting it slip through my fingers. "Because even though you want to, even though you try, you can't hate us. You can't hate me."

Anger flashed across her face, drawing her eyebrows together. "I never said I don't hate you," she spat.

"But you're not disagreeing with me," I pushed.

I knew I should have stopped. I should have given Jade space. That was what she needed. That was what she wanted.

But with every agonizing day that passed, I missed her more and more. Eventually, I wouldn't be able to stay away.

"I should hate you," she said. "I should hate you for what you did."

"Yes," I whispered, letting my fingers twirl around another strand of hair. "You *should* hate me. But you don't, do you?"

Jade's dark eyes were blazing into mine, sending a thrill of heat down my spine. Jade could lie and say she hated me. She could lie and say she didn't want to be with me.

But I knew her. There was something dark within her that I recognized. Some deep, wicked part of her called out to me. I knew she felt it, too.

"You can hate me, you know," I whispered to her, closing the distance between us slowly and letting my hand move from her hair to the nape of her neck. "If that makes it easier for you, you can hate me."

Jade's pulse moved under my thumb. Her breathing matched mine, shallow and heavy. Jade and I were different in ways I couldn't even count, but we were similar in so many, too. Being impulsive, for one. Being temperamental and wicked.

She didn't stop me as I brought my other hand to her neck, too, lifting her chin with my thumbs and bringing my lips dangerously close to hers. "Fine," she whispered back to me, letting my hands move as they pleased. "I hate you."

"You *lie*," I hissed, and then my mouth crashed into hers.

CHAPTER 7
Jade

My lips devoured his, drunk on his anger and fueled by my own emotions. I need him. I needed more.

I hate you. I hate you. I hate you.

I returned his kiss with an equally aggressive amount of passion, gripping his bare waist and pulling his body tight to mine.

It felt wrong. It felt so, so wrong.

But I couldn't stop. Malachi was everything that was wrong with me, everything that I hated.

And yet, here we were.

His hands were strong on my neck, moving my lips so he could kiss me however he liked. I wanted to be closer to him. I wanted more of him.

His hot mouth moved against mine with anger, longing, and something else.

My hands grazed the lean muscles across his back, narrowly avoiding the base of his wings.

I was dizzy, completely infatuated with Malachi.

The King of Shadows

My king.

I pushed against his chest, pulling myself away from the kiss. "Stop," I said, catching my breath. "We can't do this."

"No," he agreed, merely just to agree with me. "We can't."

But it didn't end there. I closed the distance between us this time, practically jumping into his arms and wrapping my legs around his waist. Malachi caught me with ease, resuming exactly where we had left off.

I hate you, I hate you, I hate you.

I kissed him again, our mouths becoming one as he carried me to his bed.

This was crazy. I needed to stop it.

I hate you. I hate you.

Malachi tried to lay me back, but I stopped him, flipping him over so he was the one lying on the bed, his black wings powerfully displayed on either side of him.

It was a sight that made my knees weak.

I crawled on top of him, straddling his waist and resuming our frenzy as if I had nothing to lose.

Did I have something to lose?

Do you feel lucky to be alive?

I hate you, I hate you.

I love you.

I will rip this world apart until I can place you in the sky myself, princess.

It had to stop. I had to stop this.

My mind raced through memories of him and my heart pounded just as wickedly. What in the Saints was I doing?

Do you feel lucky to be alive?

I didn't think. I couldn't. I could only act. I reached

down to my thigh, where the same dagger that Malachi had gifted me on our wedding night was strapped, and pulled it out.

And I pressed it to his throat.

Malachi stilled beneath me, a sudden cool breeze slicing the heat between us.

"Jade," he said carefully. "What are you doing?"

I knew I couldn't kill him. We both knew.

But I needed to do something. Anything. He deserved it. He *deserved* to pay for what he had done to me.

I hate you.

"Jade," he said again when I didn't reply. His hands were out in surrender at his sides. "I know you are angry. I know I deserve this. I deserve worse than this, trust me."

I realized then that tears streamed down my face, dripping one by one onto his bare chest.

"No," I muttered through gritted teeth. "You deserve... you deserve..."

I couldn't finish the thought. What *did* he deserve? He had saved my life. He was my savior and yet he was also my captor.

I was lost. I was incredibly, irrevocably lost.

I dropped the dagger, letting it fall onto the bed next to us.

And I cried.

"Oh, Jade," Malachi said, bringing his hands to my face and wiping my tears.

He sat up, wrapping his arms around me and holding me to his chest.

I cried for Tessa, for the pain she had gone through. I

cried for my father. I cried for Malachi, for everything he deserved and everything he didn't.

And I cried for myself.

Do you feel lucky to be alive?

The truth was, I didn't feel much of anything at all.

CHAPTER 8

Malachi

T wo days.

Two days since I had kissed Jade, and two days since she had spoken to me.

I didn't care. I wasn't surprised, either. Jade told me she hated me and completely fell apart in my arms.

She needed space. *Real* space this time.

But I couldn't keep wondering if she was okay. I couldn't keep worrying about her day after day.

Two days.

I couldn't wait any longer.

"Looking for something?" Adeline chirped beside me. The dining hall in the castle was crowded, I avoided it as much as possible, keeping to my own personal dining room.

But Jade had to eat. She would show up sometime.

"No," I lied. "And I'm busy."

"Right," Adeline said, completely ignoring my *busy* warning. "Jade just left," she said.

My stomach dropped.

"I wasn't looking for her," I said. "I don't care where she is."

"You're a terrible liar," she said. "You should work on that if you're going to be a convincing king."

"Do you need something, Adeline?" I asked, stopping in my tracks to face her. If Jade wasn't here, there was no use for me to linger.

"Yes," she said, tossing her hands onto her hips. "I want to check in with my brother. You've been...you've been all over the place lately. I just want to make sure you're okay."

I took a long breath. "I'm fine," I lied. "I just have a lot going on."

"And you haven't made up with Jade?" she questioned.

Saints, this woman was going to drive me over the edge. "I would prefer not to talk about her, okay?"

Adeline opened her mouth to argue, but her attention was caught by something behind me.

"Mal," she said quietly, not taking her eyes off whatever it was she was staring at. Her features morphed, one by one, from my sassy sister to a terrified girl.

I spun around, looking for what she was staring at.

And I drew my sword.

"Stop it," Jade's voice hissed through the open room. "Just calm down!"

It wasn't Jade I was worried about, though. Her father stumbled around in front of her, barely standing.

How could he possibly have gotten drunk again?

"Who the Saints is that?" Adeline whispered to me.

I fought to keep my anger at bay. Jade wouldn't want me to step in. The last time I interfered, I nearly ruined everything. "That's Jade's father," I answered.

Adeline's sharp inhale told me she was not expecting that answer.

We both approached slowly, trying to stay out of view.

"I knew this would happen!" her father spat, although the words slurred together. "You spoiled little bitch!"

I took half a step forward, but Adeline put a hand out to stop me. "Let her handle this herself," she whispered.

She was right. I knew she was.

But watching that bastard speak to my wife that way made me want to kill anyone in sight.

"You can't do this, you can't demand I stay somewhere. Take me back! Take me home!" he yelled.

"This *is* home, now," Jade whispered. Something in her voice made my chest ache. "It's for your own safety. You know this, father."

"How is living with *them* safe? How is this better? They ruined everything, Jade. They ruined it *all*."

Jade stared at her father with wide eyes, oblivious to the room of people staring at her. "Just calm down, please. I'll explain it all to you once you calm down."

Her father stumbled forward, nearly knocking Jade over. He didn't lower his voice, though. "Calm down?" he repeated. "You want me to calm down? You drag me here, with these *monsters*, and you tell *me* to calm down? That everything will be fine? That we're safe? Tell me, daughter. Do you *feel* safe?"

"We are safe here," Jade repeated. I noted her clenched fists and her tight jaw. If it weren't for Adeline standing right next to me, I would have stepped in. "These fae will protect us."

"Like your husband? Is that what he was doing when he attacked me in my own home?"

Jade stiffened.

"You don't know anything," her father pushed. "You are a young, stupid girl. You think you can save us? You think you can protect us? You're wrong. And you're ignorant." Jade began speaking but her father continued. "You are nothing special, Jade," he said. She flinched away from the spit that flew off his tongue. "You are no different than all of the other idiots who think they are so high and mighty. You're certainly not *liked* here. You think these fae *like* you? You think they will protect you? You are *nothing*. You are *nobody*. Nobody cares about you. Saints. Your own sister can't even look you in the eye."

"That's not true," Jade interrupted. She was yelling now, her face flushed red.

"It is true," her father pushed. "Did you know she had nightmares for weeks? *Weeks*. She couldn't even sleep for three hours without waking up screaming! Dreaming about *him*. Dreaming about you and him together." He paused to shake his head in disgust. "It's pathetic. Running around with these fae as if you actually mean something to them."

"Can I rip his head off now?" I whispered to Adeline.

"No," she ushered. "Jade will stop him. If you step in, she'll look weak in front of everyone."

Saints, I hated that she was right.

"Are you forgetting that this is all your fault?" Jade retorted. "I'm in this mess because of you, father. You're the one with the problem. You're the one who's pathetic. You think I wanted to be here? You think I wanted to rely on the fae for my safety? I. had. No. Choice. Did you think I *enjoyed* scaring Tessa like that? I did everything for her. *Everything!* You're the one ruining everything. You'll ruin this, too. Like you always do."

"They'll kill you," her father mumbled, no longer looking at Jade. "They'll kill us all."

"That's not true."

He spun around, spit flying into Jade's face as he yelled, "We will all die!"

My heart raced, every inch of my power wanted me to send this man to his knees. But I waited.

Jade could defend herself.

"I am the peacemaker," Jade yelled right back in his face. "I am the key to everything! You're right, father. They might kill you. Because you're a useless drunk who's good for nothing but taking up space. But me? They'll protect me with their lives. Because *I* am the key to everything."

Her father froze, as if her words triggered some sort of memory.

"The peacemaker?" he asked, barely audible.

Jade didn't answer.

"We're dead," her father spat. "We're all dead. You, me, Tessa. We'll all die. All of us."

"No!"

"YES!"

"Please stop this, father. Stop this before you make it any worse for us."

"Any worse?" he yelled after her. His tired voice echoed off the stone walls of the castle. "How could this possibly get any worse?"

"That's enough," Jade demanded.

"My own daughter has secured my death. Saints! Thank you, daughter! Thank you for ending my life!"

I felt the power before I saw it. It was a small pulse in the air, a tiny tickle in the middle of my chest. It wasn't my power, but it caused my power to stir in excitement.

The familiarity made my entire body go still.

And then I saw the tiny tendrils of magic leaving her body, ready to defend her at the single thought.

She was going to kill her father.

I rushed forward, Adeline didn't stop me this time.

"Jade," I boomed, much louder than I expected. My power rumbled through my body, shaking the few stone tables around us as I grabbed her by both shoulders.

I wasn't afraid of her hurting me. My power would protect me.

I knew it would. I felt it.

"Jade," I said again, shaking her by the shoulders. Her eyes were black pits, ready to fight for justice at the single thought.

Heat practically sizzled between us as I shook her again.

She snapped out of her daze, finally, and looked at me with wide eyes. "Saints," her father whispered behind her. "You *are* a demon!"

I twirled around, no longer able to remain quiet. "Do you remember me, Sir Farrow?"

Recognition flickered across his features. He took one step backward, almost tripping over his own feet.

"Good," I continued. "Then you know what I will do to you if you speak to Jade like that again. I don't allow anyone to disrespect my wife, Sir Farrow. I don't give a shit if you're her father or not."

He gulped.

"You're here because Jade wishes to keep her family safe. I, however, wouldn't mind hanging you from a tree and feeding the hungry monsters that lurk in the woods. So the next time you find yourself over-indulging in liquor and starting a fight with someone, it better not be my wife."

I turned my attention to the crowd of fae that now gathered, everyone wanting a front-row seat to the spectacle. "Go," I demanded. "Get out."

They obeyed.

Good.

I turned back around to Jade, who had tears swelling in her eyes.

She wouldn't let them fall, though. No, she had cried over her father one too many times.

"I'm sorry," I said to her. "I wasn't going to interrupt, but..." I glanced around us, realizing there were way too many prying ears to say what I needed to say. "Follow me," I said, grabbing Jade's arm and dragging her after me into one of the old servant rooms of the castle.

These things were starting to come in handy.

We walked down another dim, empty hallway and I pulled her into a dark room.

"Your power was out of control, Jade. I felt it first, and then I saw it. You would have killed him. You would have killed your own father."

Her eyes were wild, darting around in the darkness. "I–I had no idea. I didn't know, I was just so angry. He wouldn't stop!"

"I know," I said. "I heard it all."

"It just felt like my temper at first, it really did. I had no idea it was my power."

"How did it feel?" I asked. "Describe it to me."

"It felt...*good*. At first. Powerful. I didn't feel any different, though. I just felt strong."

I nodded, knowing the feeling all too well. "It practically radiated from your entire body. A cast of light."

"Really?" she asked. "You could see it?"

"Yes," I said. "I could. And I'm sure others could too if they paid close enough attention. This is exactly what we don't need."

"You're angry with me?" she asked.

I took a long, calming breath. How could she possibly think that? Watching Jade defend herself to her father for once was one of the best things I had witnessed in my life. That man deserved much, much worse things than death.

Even in the hands of his own daughter.

I took a step closer to Jade, who was leaning against the wall. "Of course I'm not mad," I said. "I will never be mad at you for using your power. Even if you might kill a few deserving bastards in the process."

Jade smiled. It was nice to see her smiling again. "I guess it's safe to say my power is getting stronger. It was so easy. Like my power *wanted* me to use it."

"We need to begin training again right away."

"With Esther?"

With Esther. I knew this moment would come. We couldn't leave Esther rotting away down in the dungeon forever. At some point, we were going to need her again. "Yes," I answered. "With Esther."

Jade nodded in agreement. "And what exactly will I be training for?" she asked.

"You will soon possess some of the strongest power in history, Jade. We have to teach you how to control your power, and, if needed, how to use it as your weapon."

"Do you think I will need it to defend myself?" she asked.

"I think we will be very lucky people if we never get to that point."

My gaze moved from Jade's eyes to her perfect, soft lips. In the empty room, I could practically hear each beat of her heart in her chest.

I caught myself before I made any moves I might regret. "I have to go," I said. Jade mumbled something similar. "Meet me in the garden at dusk tomorrow. We'll begin training your magic again then."

Jade barely nodded before scurrying out of the room.

"Malachi?" She stopped and called back to me.

"Yes?"

"Thank you. For defending me."

I knew Jade couldn't see it in the dark, but a smile crept onto my face. "Anytime, princess."

CHAPTER 9
Jade

"Do you think if I ran away right now and started living with the deadlings in the woods that anyone would notice?" I asked Adeline.

She smiled as she walked next to me. "I think you have a better chance at becoming king."

I smiled back. "You have your sister back. That must at least be nice, right?" she asked.

I shrugged. "It's nice knowing she's not struggling for every meal like I used to do. But...there's a different type of worry with her being here. Malachi defends us, but most of the fae still hate humans. They don't want us here. I worry that she'll see something or change the way she sees me."

"You think she'll fear you?"

"I think she fears me already."

"Because of Malachi?"

The truth was, it was *so* much more than just Malachi that frightened Tessa. It was all of it. We came from a world where it was just us two. Us and our father, who didn't really count as a whole human being.

It was terrible and dreadful and difficult every single day. But it was constant. It was a painful type of comfort.

Tessa had grown to know a version of me that was defiant and scrappy. Before I was sold to marry Malachi, I would have laughed at anyone who tried to tell me what to do. Who tried to tell me who to be.

Tessa saw that. She was there every time, watching her big sister rip through this world with no regrets.

Who was I now? The human girl who walked on ice around the fae? They certainly didn't fear me. No, they *never* would.

I would *never* be their equal. Even with Adeline.

Adeline still waited for my reply. I wasn't going to lie to her. She had become a great friend to me over our time together. And I knew she would understand.

"Partly because of Malachi," I started. "But I think she will fear who I have become, too."

"The wife to the King of Shadows?" she asked.

A chill ran down my spine at her words, even in the warmth of the evening. King of Shadows. "No," I corrected. "She'll fear me because I am broken."

"Oh, Jade," she stared. "I think we're all a little broken. You, me, Malachi. Even Tessa. It's what makes us sane."

I smiled at her kind words. "You think we're all sane?"

"Well," she retorted. "To be honest, I think you and I may be the only ones."

I shook my head at her as we came to the clearing of the lagoon, the same lagoon where we had been attacked by a *tiger* of all things.

"It seems different here," I noticed. The large lagoon with the beautiful blue water seemed hardly larger than a pond now. The forest around the clearing looked half as threatening.

"That's because you're different, now," she said. "Saints, it feels like a lifetime ago when I brought you here the first time."

"Do you think Malachi will be just as pissed if he finds us here again?"

"Please," she said, tossing her long hair over her shoulder. "We can take care of ourselves."

Something stirred in my chest at her words. She was right. I had changed since I had been here last.

But so had she.

She wasn't the ditsy, naive girl I had taken her for when I first met her. Adeline was strong in ways I would never have to understand.

I silently thanked the Saints for that.

"Are you going for a swim?" she asked me.

"I think I'll pass this time," I replied. "I still have night-mares about those freaky kraken trying to drown me."

Adeline's face lit up, as if just now remembering the attack. "Saints, Jade! I'm so sorry! Oh my, I'm such an idiot for bringing you out here!"

"Adeline!" I said, grabbing her by her shoulders to calm her down. "It's okay. I have much worse things to be afraid of. Truly. Swimming just...I think I'll take a break from leisurely dips in the pond for a while."

She seemed to relax under my touch. "Fine," she said. "I can't believe I forgot about that."

"Don't worry," I said. "Lifetimes ago. Remember?"

She smiled softly. "So, have you spoken to Sadie at all?"

I snapped my attention to her, noting the directness of the question. "Why do you ask?"

She shrugged. "No reason. A little birdie just happened to tell me you like to lurk in the dungeons from time to time."

I rolled my eyes. "Malachi has such a big mouth."

"Oh, please," she spat. "I basically had to pry it out of him. He doesn't talk to me much at all these days."

"Yeah," I agreed. "That makes two of us."

Silence filled the air between us. I turned my attention to the nature that surrounded us. To my right, a bright red butterfly landed on a small yellow flower that bloomed from the wall of green shrubbery. Birds chirped lightly in the distance, just loud enough to add the ambiance of the flowing water. The sun glistened through the tall tree branches above.

"He misses you," she interrupted.

"What?"

"Malachi. He misses you. It's killing him that you two aren't together."

Heat rose to my cheeks. "Did he tell you that?" I asked, pretending to look around at the trees.

"He didn't have to. It's pretty obvious, Jade. But I know you know that, too."

I paused for a moment, considering her words. "I can't just forgive him, Adeline. He...he *betrayed* me."

"Look," she said, turning to face me. "I love you, so I'm going to be honest with you. Malachi didn't betray you. Not even close. He saved your life, just like he has done dozens of times before. And then he broke the treaty to go retrieve your family so that you might have a tiny chance at not hating him for once. He did not betray you, Jade. You just saw a different side of him than he had once shown you."

"I didn't like that side of him," I said, but something dark inside of me resisted the words. *Liar.* "He's dangerous."

"Yes, he is. And do you want to know the crazy part?"

"Sure," I sighed.

"When your power becomes stronger, which after what I saw in the dining hall tonight is already happening, you'll be just as dangerous."

Just as dangerous as the King of Shadows?

"That's not possible."

"It is possible, Jade. Malachi loves you. What would you do to protect the people you love? Where would you draw the line? I bet pretending to trade Malachi's life for your own doesn't even come close to the ends you would go to. What if it were Tessa?"

"But it wasn't Tessa. It was me."

"Yes, it was. You're strong, Jade. And you're his. You'll always be his, and he'll kill anyone who touches you. You know this is true."

I shrugged. "He still hasn't killed Isaiah, though, has he?"

"He will when the time is right," she said.

"You really defend him a lot, you know."

"Yes, I do. And it's not just because I love him. He's right. He is strong and gracious, yet terrifying and merciless. You can trust him, Jade. You can forgive him."

I finally looked Adeline in the eye. "If I forgive him, then what am I? How will Tessa look at me then? How will my father?"

Adeline huffed and propped her hands onto her hips. "I'm not going to pretend for one second that I give two shits about your father, Jade. But Tessa? She loves you, too. As long as you're okay, she'll find a way to forgive you for anything."

I spent the rest of the evening thinking about my time with Adeline. Saints, I hated how she was always right. Her and Malachi, both.

I needed to forgive him. If not for his sake, then for my own.

I laid in bed, staring at the dark ceiling above me. The castle was just as beautiful as I had remembered, I had to admit that much. Green vines looped in and out of the stones, creating a maze of nature that kept my mind at bay.

Until I heard a small knock on my door.

It wasn't Malachi. The knocking was too light.

I got out of bed and padded silently over to the door. Before I could say anything, my visitor knocked again.

More desperate this time.

"Who is it?" I asked.

"Jade!" Tessa's voice whispered through the night. "Jade, let me in!"

Saints.

I grabbed my door and flung it open. Tessa stumbled in, out of breath.

"What's going on?" I asked, scanning her body from head to toe in the darkness. "Are you hurt?"

"No, no," she ushered. "I'm fine. I came to see you."

"How did you find me here?"

"Please," she shrugged. "You have to give me some credit."

I huffed, placing my hands on my hips. "You can't be wandering around the fae castle at night, Tessa. It isn't safe."

"I wasn't going to stay locked up like a prisoner with him any more, Jade. I couldn't!"

She was talking about our father.

"What did you do to him?" she asked. "He was practically carried back to our room, completely disheveled."

I turned and walked to my open window. "You mean more than the usual?" I asked.

Tessa walked in and sat on my bed as if she lived there, too. "He's completely lost his mind, Jade. He's been mumbling on and on about mother."

My heart stopped. "Our mother?"

"Yes!"

I moved to sit next to her, fighting to keep any signs of alarm off my face.

"What's he been saying?"

Tessa shrugged. "Nothing I can understand. He's been rambling about you, saying something like 'he remembers'. When I ask what it is that he remembers, he shuts down."

Our father must have known something. I had been wondering this ever since Esther whispered about knowing my mother.

They had to have known. They had to have known that I was supposed to be special.

"We can't trust anything he says," I reminded her. "He's lost."

She looked at me with deep, glazed eyes. "I've never seen him like this before," she said. "It's like he's fighting himself."

Maybe he was fighting himself. Maybe he knew more than he had ever admitted. Maybe deep down, he had buried the truth in an ocean of liquor and never looked back.

Either way, it didn't matter now.

I crawled under my covers and patted the spot next to me,

inviting Tessa to do the same. "He'll calm down soon," I said. "Being away from home has to be hard for him, too."

Tessa curled up next to me. "Do you remember her?" she asked after a few beats of silence.

I took a long breath, trying to recall any memories of my mother.

"No," I answered honestly. "Although sometimes I see a tall, beautiful woman in my dreams. I like pretending that's her."

Tessa giggled. "I think it might be."

I waited until her breathing slowed down, and I let my eyes shut.

Maybe I would see her again.

CHAPTER 10

Malachi

"I can't just *summon* it like you can," Jade said. "I don't know how it happened. It was instinct."

"Exactly," I said. "Instinct. Your body knows what to do. Your power knows what to do. Listen to those things."

She huffed and closed her eyes again.

I had dragged her out of the castle into the safety of the forest. That way, she wouldn't accidentally burn the castle down if things went wrong.

But at the rate we were moving, the only thing burning down was my patience.

"Try harder," I demanded.

"You can't just bark at me to use magic and think that will work, Mal," she said. I had to admit, seeing her sass me again nearly put a smile on my face. It was a step up from her usual act of ignoring me.

"Fine," I said. "What do you want me to do?"

"Just...just *wait.*"

"I can wait," I said.

"Good. And be quiet."

I nodded, taking the hint, and backed up a few paces to give her some space.

"The two times I used my power I felt...I felt desperate. I felt helpless."

I continued to stay silent.

"But I don't want to feel desperate. I want to feel powerful."

Jade placed her hands on her stomach as if to center herself. As if to feel the power that lived there.

My own power tickled with excitement. I took a deep, calming breath to settle it.

It was an interesting thought—that my dark, murderous power recognized whatever power was blooming inside of Jade.

By the time I turned my attention back to Jade, she was looking at me with her hands on her hips. "It's not working."

I signed. "It never will work if you keep thinking that way."

"You know what we need to do," she said. "We need her."

Esther. "No, we don't."

"She can teach me how to use this."

"We can't trust her, Jade!"

"Maybe not. But if she needs me like she says she does, she has every interest to develop my magic as quickly as possible. You know it's true."

Saints. Yes, I did know it was true.

But I hadn't confronted Esther since Trithen. I didn't want to do it now.

Jade stepped forward, close enough that I thought she might reach out and touch me.

She didn't.

"I know you're afraid," she said.

"What?"

"You're afraid to confront your mother."

"That's not true," I said. *Why did I feel defensive?*

"She has no power here, Mal. She can't do anything to you. She can't hurt me, either. You won't let her."

I unclenched my tight fists and tried to relax. "It's not getting hurt that I'm worried about."

"Then what? What's keeping you from walking into that dungeon right now and demanding that Esther helps us?"

I turned and paced in the grassy garden. What was stopping me? If Esther so much as looked at Jade or myself the wrong way, I would end her.

So why was I resisting?

Jade walked up behind me, placing her delicate hands on my back. My wings flared in response, but Jade didn't back away. "Hey," she whispered, dangerously close. "I'll be with you the whole time."

Jade hadn't forgiven me. I knew that. This didn't change anything.

She wanted to learn her magic just as badly as we needed her to learn it.

Yet somehow, her touch on my bare skin sent a thrill of delight down my spine. "Fine," I said, clearing my throat.

"Fine?"

"If you want to speak with Esther so badly, we'll go."

Jade's face lit up. "Really? Right now?"

I nodded, and she practically jumped with joy.

"But I do the talking. And if she even tries to touch you, I'll kill her."

"I don't doubt that for a second."

And then we were on our way, marching through the grass to visit my mother in the dungeons of Rewyth.

CHAPTER 11
Jade

Malachi's body stiffened as we descended the stairs into the dungeon. Chills rose on my arms, and I knew it wasn't entirely from the sudden drop in temperature.

"You're sure about this?" I asked him as we continued to descend.

"It's better to get it over with now," he answered coldly.

I nodded. Fair enough.

I had come down to the dungeons a handful of times since we had been back to Rewyth, but never to see Esther. Or Isaiah, for that matter. I had cared about Sadie, and that was it.

No, I didn't care about Esther.

Esther was none of my business.

She tried to kill Malachi. The thought alone put a fire in my heart.

Her own son.

I was glad Malachi walked ahead of me. That way, he couldn't see the flash of anger that came over me.

I wanted to kill her. I wanted to be the reason that witch left this place for good.

Malachi deserved better. Even with all of the terrible things he had done, he deserved better.

Malachi led us through the maze of tunnels in the dark underearth. It continued to get darker and darker, with lanterns of fire spaced out more and more as we continued.

"How far back did you chain her up?" I asked, half-joking.

"She deserved worse," he said.

I followed him in silence until we walked to the near end of the dungeons. A guard perched just outside of a cell. Her cell, from what I assumed.

"King Malachi," the guard announced. He stood from his wooden stool so quickly that it nearly fell over behind him as he began brushing his uniform with his hands. "What a pleasure."

"Leave us," was all Malachi said.

The guard obeyed without another thought, scurrying into the darkness.

"You have a visitor," Malachi barked into the cell.

In the dim light, it was hard to make out anything far away. But I squinted my eyes, and within a few seconds, I could see a small figure huddled to the stone ground in the back of the cell.

Esther.

She lifted her head at the sound of Mal's voice.

"Malachi," she acknowledged. "Come to finish the job?"

Malachi huffed a laugh, but I could feel how tense he was standing right next to me.

"You won't get off that easily, *mother.*"

She attempted to move, but heavy chains held her down to the ground. They looked ridiculous on her tiny, boney body. But I knew, deep down, she was dangerous.

Too dangerous to be freed of her chains.

"I'm training my magic," I said, interrupting them before their feud could continue. Esther seemed to notice me standing there for the first time. Her hair was matted around her neck, and her linen clothes were covered in dirt. I pretended not to notice. "I figured you could be of use."

"Interesting," she nodded. "So you've come for my help finally?"

"We don't need your help," Malachi interrupted.

"Your bride says differently, son."

I stuck my hand out, cutting Malachi off before he continued. "We have no problem leaving you in here for the next decade, *witch,* but if you would like to offer your insight to training my powers to develop, we would accept it."

She opened her mouth to respond, but a coughing fit was the only thing that came out.

Saints. She wasn't going to last much longer down here. In the corner of my eye, I saw Malachi's jaw tighten.

"Will you unchain me?" she asked after a few seconds.

Malachi spoke up first, "Absolutely not."

"Mal," I hissed under my breath. If Esther was going to agree to work with us, we had to give her something. Otherwise, she had no benefit in this deal.

Malachi snapped his attention to me. I could see his furrowed brows in the darkness. "We're not letting her out of here."

"We don't have to," I whispered back. "Just unchain her. She won't get far, anyway. Look at her."

We both looked to where Esther still huddled on the stone.

She was decaying. She was half the woman she was in Trithen.

Did I feel bad? No, I didn't feel bad. A tiny, hidden part of myself actually delighted in her suffering.

That was the part that kept me alive.

That was the part of me that didn't feel sorry for those who had wronged me.

"Fine," Malachi sighed. He walked forward with the keys from the guard and knelt before Esther. I watched as he picked up each of her wrists that were buried in the heap of metal chains, and unlocked them.

After the chains rattled to the stone ground, he stood and backed away.

Esther moved to get up from her spot in the corner, but struggled to stand. I glanced at Malachi, who only tightened his jaw. I would have to do this myself. I took the few steps into the cell and grabbed ahold of her arm, lifting her to her feet.

"Thank you, child," she whispered. I knew Malachi would be mad that I helped her. That I touched her. But this woman was clearly nothing more than helpless.

"I almost lost control of my power earlier," I explained to her after I was a safe distance way. "But I haven't been able to summon it since then."

She nodded. "What were you doing when you almost lost control?"

"I was fighting with my father," I said.

Esther nodded, recognition flickering in her eyes. "Your family is here? In Rewyth?"

"Enough talking," Malachi interrupted. "Help her with her magic."

Esther signed, but eventually turned her attention back to me. "Show me."

I held my hands out in front of me, as if somehow envisioning power between my palms would actually make it appear.

We all waited for a few seconds. I tried to think about how angry I was when my father called me useless. How embarrassing it was for me to be humiliated in front of everyone.

I thought about Tessa, and about how terrified she would be to see this.

And I thought of Malachi. And how he was trying everything possible to keep me alive.

Yet still, I felt nothing. I felt no power.

I dropped my hands to my sides with a strong exhale. "Nothing," I explained. "I feel nothing."

Esther glanced between me and Malachi, suspicion in her eyes.

"What?" I asked.

"You didn't feel anything," she explained, "but he did."

Malachi uncrossed his arms from where he stood at the entrance of the cell. "What are you talking about?" he spat.

"I'm talking about the fact that you can feel her power. You can recognize it. Can't you?"

Malachi opened his mouth, and I half-expected him to curse at Esther for having such a ridiculous accusation.

But he said nothing and closed his mouth.

Could he feel my power?

I took a step closer to him, leaving Esther behind me.

"Mal?" I asked. I called to my power, imagining what it would be like to wield it. To be powerful.

Malachi took a deep breath and closed his eyes.

My stomach dropped. "You can feel this," I whispered.

He opened his eyes, and his gaze blared into me with a heat that sent a fire down my spine.

"It's not *me* that feels it," he finally admitted. "It's my power."

"Like calls to like, darlings," Esther said from behind. "Your magic recognizes hers."

"How is that possible?" I asked her. "It's just power. How can it recognize anything?"

Esther shrugged. "I've heard of this happening. You two are so close, Malachi's mature magic has come to recognize when yours is close. His power either recognizes yours as a threat...or an ally."

I didn't dare look at Malachi, but I knew he was already staring at me.

Our powers were somehow connected.

But that wasn't going to help me learn to call it.

"How does this help me?" I said, cutting off the conversation. "Teach me how to call my power forward."

Esther took a long, shaking breath. "You were angry with your father when it came to you?"

"Yes."

"Good."

"Good?"

"Yes. You just need to get angry again."

"I've already tried that," I answered. "It didn't work."

"Well, you're in the depths of the dungeons of Rewyth," Esther replied. "Perhaps it will be different this time."

Yeah, right.

"Just try it," Malachi barked, still standing near the entrance.

"Fine," I mumbled. I closed my eyes and focused on anger.

The one emotion I had felt too much of lately.

Anger.

My father came to mind first, naturally. I did feel angry. I felt angry about the way he treated me.

But not angry enough.

Why was I *really* angry? Was it the things my father yelled at me? All of those nasty words?

He had called me trash. He had called me selfish and stupid. Did those things make me angry enough to call my power forward?

I didn't think so.

What else did he say? What else was he yelling at me in the dining hall?

The fae. He talked about the fae, about how they would never keep me safe.

That they would kill me the first chance they got.

My heart rate sped up.

He talked about how Malachi would never protect me.

I clenched my fists.

I didn't outright defend the fae. I wasn't one of them.

But...I had partially defended them, hadn't I? By not hating them, I was defending them.

In Fearford I defended them to the humans. In Trithen I defended them to the other fae.

Because they were...they were my family when my family was nothing.

A bead of sweat formed at the nape of my neck, even in the chill of the dungeons.

Is that what made me angry? The fact that I had fought so hard to defend these fae and my father just ran in here and slandered them all?

After all they had done for me?

My mind flipped.

After all they had done to me...

Yes, I defended them. But Malachi was the one that held my life at knifepoint.

Tessa's voice haunted my thoughts.

Do you feel lucky to be alive?

"Jade," Malachi's soft voice pierced through the voice in my head. "Jade, open your eyes."

I did what I was told, and my jaw dropped.

In front of me, between my hands and glowing bright red, was a ball of my power.

"Saints," I muttered. "Holy Saints."

"Good," Esther said. "Now more."

"More?" I breathed. "More what?"

"More power. Breathe into it. Release."

I took a deep breath, and to my surprise, the red ball in front of me grew.

Malachi stepped forward, finally entering back into the cell. "How dangerous is it?" he asked Esther.

"Why don't we find out," she answered.

Before I had time to process what was happening, Esther grabbed my wrist and pushed, flinging my ball of power directly toward Malachi.

My heart dropped. A scream echoed through the stone walls.

My scream.

"Malachi," I breathed, finally forcing myself to look at him, at the damage I had caused.

But when I opened my eyes, Malachi was standing just as he was before.

Totally fine.

"What happened?" I asked. "How are you not hurt?"

Malachi's mouth was slightly open, as if he was just as shocked by my power not hurting him.

"I didn't feel a thing," Malachi said. "I'm fine, Jade."

Esther laughed under her breath. "Jade can block your power," she said, "and you can block hers. What a sight."

"What? What does that mean?" I asked. An emotion I didn't even understand bubbled in my chest.

"I don't know," Esther breathed, "but whatever it is, you two should stick together. It can't be a bad thing that you are both immune to each other's power."

I was breathing heavily now, unable to slow down my heart rate. I still didn't understand my power, the damage it could cause.

It had completely disintegrated that cage of bones in Trithen, turning the entire thing, deadling with it, to ash.

Malachi's power was pain. Plain and simple. With a single thought, Malachi could drop an army of men to their knees.

I had seen it with my own eyes.

But my power was so *tangible*. It had been right there, sitting in my hands.

It was *different*.

Yet powerful. I felt the power now, calling to me. It was more familiar than it was the last time.

I knew my power could destroy that deadling, but what else could it do? Was there a limit to my power?

Was there a limit to anyone's?

Or was my power just as destructive as what it had done to that cage? Would my power disintegrate anyone it touched?

We ran through the exercise again and again. Malachi and Esther both watched as I drew that ball of power time and time again until exhaustion overtook my body.

I kept my eyes away from Malachi as much as possible, but I couldn't deny the increasing heat in my chest at the thought of his power recognizing mine.

The King of Shadows, indeed.

CHAPTER 12
Jade

I let the maids fill my bath with scorching hot water. As hot as possible, I told them.

They only looked slightly concerned with my request.

"You may go," I demanded once the bath was full, steam radiating off the surface.

They both nodded and scurried away.

My towel fell to the floor. I walked to sit on the edge of the bath. My hand shook as I reached out, feeling the steaming surface.

And then I dipped it in.

The water felt hot, yes, but not in a painful way. The scorching water comforted me, warming the coldest parts of my soul.

I let my body sink fully into the water, my heart rate immediately slowing down in relaxation. I closed my eyes and leaned my head against the back of the bath.

Saints. Months ago, I was a normal girl. Now, I was a peacemaker with magic?

When would I finally wake up from the nightmare of my life?

The scorching water cooled with every passing second. My eyelids grew heavy, fighting to stay open.

After a few minutes, I let them close.

Until I heard footsteps approaching in the darkness.

Malachi's figure appeared in the doorway of the bathroom.

"Saints," I mumbled. "What are you doing here?"

"I had to see you."

"I'm kind of occupied right now, Malachi!"

"I'll be quick," he said, completely ignoring my objections and walking into the bathroom. "I promise."

I leaned back into the water, suddenly extremely grateful that the room was dimly lit.

"What's so important that you couldn't wait until I was *clothed*?"

Malachi crossed his arms and leaned against the bathroom wall. The shadows of the corner covered the expressions of his face, and his black wings were tucked tightly behind his shoulders. "Us," was all he said.

"What do you mean?"

Malachi lifted his eyes and stared at the ceiling, lost in thought.

"If you're talking about our magic, I don't think—"

"Not just our magic, Jade," he said, pushing himself from the wall and approaching the bathtub.

I tensed, but I didn't stop him.

He kneeled next to the tub but his eyes didn't leave mine. "I've known you were different from the moment I saw you, Jade. I could just...*feel* it. But not just me. I've felt something more than simply whatever this is between us, Jade. After today, it all makes sense."

My blood stilled. "What makes sense?"

"My power recognizes you, Jade. It calls for you. When you used your magic today, I could feel it electrifying my entire body."

"But why?" I asked. "Does that happen when you're around others with magic?"

"Never," he said. "I've spent years with the Paragon, each of them possessing a gift similar to ours. I've never felt anything like this."

I shook my head, trying to make sense of his words. "Well...what does that mean?"

"I don't know," he answered. "But as crazy as this sounds, I think we were meant to find each other in this life, Jade Farrow."

"Weyland," I corrected, shocked that I even said the word.

"What?"

"It's Jade Weyland."

An emotion I couldn't name flashed across his face in the dim room before he quickly covered it up, clenching his jaw and clearing his throat.

"Whatever you say, Jade Weyland," he added.

I didn't try to hide my own smile.

As much as I hated what had transpired between me and Mal, I *was* his wife. Sometime in the chaos of our lives together, I had accepted that.

There was no going back.

Even if I did pretend to hate him.

Malachi let his arm fall over the edge of the tub, his fingers barely touching the surface of the now-barely warm water.

I froze.

His fingers moved toward my shoulder, tracing the outline of my upper arm in the water.

"Beautiful," he muttered.

The sudden compliment nearly made my jaw drop. He turned his attention back to my eyes, and I saw the deep longing that swarmed beneath them.

My heart twisted.

"Malachi," I whispered. I wasn't sure what I was going to say next. I wasn't sure what I wanted. But I did know what I felt.

I felt pulled to Malachi in ways that were indescribable.

He must have known, too. He moved his hand up to my neck, cupping my chin. "I know you hate me, Jade. I know I've ruined everything. I deserve this. I deserve you ignoring me. But..."

I found myself leaning into his touch. "But what?"

"I can't stay away from you, Jade. I can't. I tried to give you space. I tried to leave you alone. But all I can think about every second of every day is how amazing your lips taste, and how much I need you in my life."

Fire erupted in my stomach. I knew Malachi wanted me. That wasn't exactly a secret between us.

But saying it this way...

I was about to respond when a loud siren wailed through the air. Malachi stood up instantly, looking out the window.

Still naked in the bathtub, I froze, adrenaline already pounding through my body.

"What is that?" I asked.

Malachi's wings flared on either side of his body.

"Malachi," I repeated. "What is that sound?"

Malachi moved to the edge of the room and grabbed my towel, tossing it to me. "Get dressed," he demanded.

I obeyed immediately, standing from the tub and wrapping myself in the towel.

"Tell me," I yelled. "What's happening?"

Malachi spun around and closed the distance between us, grabbing hold of my shoulders tightly. "That's the warning siren," he said. "We're being attacked."

CHAPTER 13
Malachi

The castle of Rewyth had been attacked twice in my lifetime.

And twice, I had assisted in killing every single enemy that approached us.

Victory was not a question. Death for our attackers was not a question.

Still. That didn't stop my body from going into full-on *war* mode. Every single muscle tensed with adrenaline, ready to protect this kingdom at all costs.

Ready to protect Jade at all costs.

Jade finished getting dressed in the bathroom as I took a deep breath, trying to clear my thoughts.

It could have been a test, I told myself. It's entirely possible that this was just a test, or a mistake by whomever blew the siren.

Something inside of me knew that wasn't true, though.

The pit in my stomach told me that the siren rang true.

We were under attack.

Jade emerged from the bathroom wearing leather trousers

and a tunic. It wasn't perfect battle attire, but it was better than a long skirt.

"Let's go," I demanded, sticking my hand out. She grabbed it without hesitating, and I pulled her into the halls of the castle.

Immediate chaos filled the halls. Guards were running in every direction, trying to figure out the best way to defend our castle.

They needed guidance from their king.

"To the gates!" I shouted. My voice echoed off the stone walls, and every single person in hearing range halted. "Defend the front gates!"

And then everyone began running. I pulled Jade tightly to my side and began running along with everyone else.

I needed to figure out what was threatening us. Once I found that out, I could decide how to protect Jade.

That's what mattered. Protect Jade. Protect the castle.

Jade stayed silent as we weaved through the castle walls. I pulled her through the front doors, ducking to the corner as everyone else continued to push forward to the front gates.

"Mal," Serefin's voice rang from behind me. I held Jade's hand tighter as I spun around.

"Serefin," I greeted. "Tell me what's happening."

"They came out of nowhere," he said, out of breath. "There are dozens, Mal. Dozens of them."

My stomach dropped. I knew exactly what Serefin was talking about.

Jade stepped even closer to my side. "What is it?" she asked.

"Deadlings," Serefin and I answered at the same time. I

looked at Jade, who only showed the shock in the wideness of her eyes. "We're being attacked by deadlings."

Guards continued to rush toward the gates.

"We aren't surrounded yet," Serefin informed me. "But they keep coming out of the forest."

"What do they want?" Jade asked. "Why are they coming here?"

Serefin gave me a knowing look. "They're being controlled by something or someone," I answered Jade. "But they sure as shit won't make it past these walls. Serefin, take command of the gates. You know what to do. I'll get Jade somewhere safe and I'll be back."

Serefin nodded and was gone in the blink of an eye.

Now, it was time to get rid of Jade.

"Let's go," I said, turning to pull her back inside the castle.

"What?" she asked. "No! I can help!"

"Absolutely not," I barked. "You're going somewhere safe where I don't have to worry about you."

Jade resisted, but I pulled her hand even harder, causing her to stumble forward after me.

I didn't care. I would throw her over my shoulder kicking and screaming if I had to. She would not face this battle.

"Mal!" she yelled. "I'm not a helpless child! I can help!"

"I'm taking you to the dungeons," I demanded. The dungeons were deep enough in the castle, that even if a few deadlings breached our walls, they would never find Jade.

They would never make it that far.

"The dungeons?!" Jade yelled, panic arising in her voice. "You can't leave me down there, Mal!"

This girl.

I spun Jade around and pinned her to the wall. Others still rushed behind us, but I didn't care if anyone saw.

"I'm going to tell you this once, so you better listen up. I'm very aware that you can defend yourself. I'm very aware that you are not a child, Jade. But those deadlings will stop at nothing. They will kill and kill and kill until there is nothing left. You've seen a couple of deadlings in your life, but an army? This is entirely different. You won't last out there, Jade. And even if you could, I can't think of a single damned thing knowing you might be in danger. So shut up, and follow me. Because I need to defend my castle, and I can't do that if I have to look for you over my shoulder every damned second!"

Jade opened her mouth to reply, but quickly shut it. "Fine," was all she said.

"Good. Now let's go."

Within two minutes, we were at the entrance of the dungeon. The guards that normally guarded the tunnels were gone, all called to defend the walls of Rewyth.

"Stay hidden," I said to her. "Wait for me to come get you."

I didn't wait to see if she kept moving. I turned on my heels and ran as fast as I could to defend the walls of my castle.

CHAPTER 14
Jade

Malachi truly did not know me at all if he thought I was going to sit quietly in the dungeons while he fought to defend this castle.

As soon as he was out of sight, I ran in the direction of the servants' quarters, where I knew Tessa would be hiding.

At least I *hoped* she was still there.

I bursted through Malachi's personal dining room, remembering which door led to the secret hallway.

I had no problem finding it this time, fueled by adrenaline and a desperate need to find my sister.

"Tessa?" I yelled as I slowly pushed the door open. "Tessa, are you in here?"

"Jade!" she answered, slamming herself into my chest. I hugged her back, thanking the Saints that she was still here. "What's happening?" she asked. "We heard the siren, but I–"

"We're being attacked," I answered quickly.

"What?" she asked, eyes wild. "By who?"

"It's not exactly a *who*," I started explaining before I realized that Tessa would have no idea what a deadling was.

People back home... they didn't know about those things. I had only recently found out what a deadling was.

And that was when I had been *attacked* by one.

"It doesn't matter," I quickly recovered. "I just want to know that you're safe. Is father here?"

Tessa stepped aside, motioning to our father who was still somehow passed out on the bed.

No surprise there.

I gripped Tessa's shoulders and bent down so that I was looking directly into her eyes. "I need you to stay here, Tessa. No matter what happens, I need you to stay in this room until I come get you. Do you understand?"

"Where are you going?"

"I have to take care of something," I answered. "I'll be safe. I just need to know you're safe, too. Do you promise you won't leave?"

Tessa nodded frantically.

"Good," I said. "It will be over soon." I kissed her forehead and was gone, the small wooden door closing behind me.

And then I was moving.

I had been trained for war personally by Malachi himself.

I could handle a few deadlings.

The knife I always wore was strapped tightly to my thigh, ready to be wielded. Adrenaline pulsed through my veins, but it was a calm rush. I knew what I needed to do.

I was focused. I was ready.

Most of the halls were empty now, allowing me to sneak back to the front doors of the castle without being noticed.

Serefin's voice commanding the front line became audible as I crept closer.

My power practically buzzed beneath the surface of my skin.

If these deadlings were attacking the castle, they likely had a target.

I wasn't going to sit back and wait for them to find me.

My feet bounced over the ground as I crept closer to the wall, closer to the fight.

I knew there was an opening at the–

"I'm more than certain Malachi didn't approve of this." Serefin's voice cut through my thoughts. *Shit.*

He stormed forward and grabbed me by the arm. "Let's go. You're getting out of here."

"I can help, Ser!"

"No! You can't! Now get back inside before you cause more trouble!" He spoke to me in a voice I had never heard of coming from him. It was stern enough to shut me up. Serefin had always been kind to me, but I wasn't in any position to get on his bad side.

His fae strength forced me away from the gate.

"Serefin!" Malachi whispered in the darkness, just around the corner. "Serefin, where did you–"

He was cut off by the sight of us.

"Jade?"

"Don't be mad!" I yelled. "I only want to help!"

"Serefin, go finish them off. The numbers are dwindling. Make sure there are no more hidden in the trees," Malachi demanded. Serefin nodded and ran into the darkness.

Mal grabbed my arm where Ser had just let go, dragging me in the same direction. "What were you thinking?"

"I was thinking I could blast some of those damn deadlings with my power, just like I did in Trithen!"

Malachi yanked my arm again. "And you didn't stop to realize how ridiculously stupid that plan was?"

"Wanting to help my *husband* in *war* is not stupid!"

He stopped walking to face me. "First of all, this is not war. This was an irresponsible attack sent to shake us up. Likely to see what power we had hiding behind these walls. If you were to walk out there and blast them all away with your magic, we would have given away our one secret to whichever one of our enemies is behind this."

Shit. I hadn't thought of that.

"I know you want to help," Malachi said.

"I do!"

"Then please do the kingdom a favor, and stay inside."

He pushed me toward the castle and stormed away, not bothering to look back.

Malachi had spoken to me like that dozens of times, but this time, his words stung more than usual.

He was my king. I knew that. But he was also my husband.

Did he not see that I was reaching out? That I was trying?

The sounds of the attacks from the deadlings dwindled with every second.

I snuck back inside and headed straight for my bedroom. Anywhere else would be no good.

Malachi didn't see me as his equal. He didn't see me as a strong partner that could help him rule this kingdom.

He saw me as a child he still had to protect.

I waited up until I couldn't hear a single clash of metal through my open window.

This fight was over.

But this was only the beginning of war.

T had just dozed off into sleep when Malachi knocked. I could tell it was him right away—he knocked like it pained him to do so.

I stood up and secured my robe around my waist before shuffling to let him in.

"Are you alright?" he asked as he shut the door behind him.

"Shouldn't I be asking you that question?" I examined him closely, running my eyes over all of the splattered blood that stained his skin. I grabbed his chin and tilted his face to the side, looking for any sign of injury.

"I'm okay," he said quietly. "The blood isn't mine."

A breath of air escaped me as I let my hands fall back to my sides. "Good."

I turned my back to him and walked further into my bedroom. My feet chilled against the cool, hard floor.

"You scared me half to death, you know," Malachi continued. "Seeing you out there wasn't exactly calming."

I tilted my head back and stared at the dark ceiling. "I was only trying to help," I admitted under my breath.

Malachi approached behind me. The shadow of his wings illuminated on the wall. "I know you were," he said just as lightly.

I spun to face him. "Then why not let me? Why not let me assist the people who are saving my life?"

"They were just fine without you," he said. He took another step closer.

"Well, that makes me feel very valuable. Thanks."

A bloodied hand came up to tug on the bottom of my

hair. "There is nothing more precious to me in this entire kingdom, Jade. I'm sorry I lashed out at you, but..."

"But what?"

His eyes darkened. "I can't think straight knowing you are in danger. I can't... I can't–"

I interrupted him by placing both hands on his face. "I know," was all I said. He closed his eyes under my touch. I rubbed my thumbs lightly over his chiseled cheekbones before saying, "You're covered in blood. Let me help you."

Malachi let me pull him to the dimly lit bathroom in my room. Silence lingered between us as I dampened a cloth and returned to where he leaned against the doorframe.

When he reached for the cloth, I stopped him. "Let me do it," I whispered.

He nodded.

Malachi bowed his head under my touch. He let me clean the blood and dirt from his skin in silence until the sun began to rise.

When he suggested he needed to return to his own room, I didn't stop him.

But I couldn't shake the feeling that washed over me when I saw the pained look in his eyes as he went.

CHAPTER 15
Malachi

The tithe happened at the beginning of every season. My father used to say it was for the purpose of "receiving what was rightfully owed to the castle".

I had no idea what he meant by that, but the tithes continued, regardless. Year after year, members of Rewyth lined up, ready to offer anything they could as payment to the kingdom.

In return, the King would offer his good graces.

Sometimes the citizens would even hand over their first-born children, they were so desperate to be seen as noble.

I tried not to actively grimace as I entered the throne room. This was never a room that I liked. It only reminded me of greed.

But that was my fathers reign. All of those terrible memories, all of those moments of brutality that took place on these very stone floors.

That reign was in the past.

I was here to create new memories. New reign. New power.

My heels clicked the shining floor as I walked up the stone stairs and took a seat on the throne that was now nearly overgrown with vines and greenery from the surrounding walls.

I tried to settle in, to relax. The tithe was beneficial to the kingdom, that much held true no matter who sat in this throne. But it also had benefits for the citizens. They had the opportunity to be seen. To have their problems and grievances heard.

Of course, those *problems* were rarely handled without bloodshed in this very room while my father reigned.

"Let us know when you're ready," Serefin said from the front doors of the room. A small nod of encouragement came soon after, small enough that only I would see.

I took a long breath. This was my first tithe as a king. This was my first opportunity to give everyone the impression of who I was and what I was made of.

It was time these people had peace here in Rewyth. *Real* peace.

But at the same time, I wasn't going to let anyone threaten my position as King of Rewyth.

The golden crown I wore felt heavier than it looked. It cut into my skin at my ears, not helping my irritated mood in the slightest.

"Let them in," I ordered Ser. He nodded and, with the help of another guard, pulled the massive doors open.

I held my breath and waited.

The first citizen to enter was a young fae, maybe a decade old.

His silver wings were still small, yet they flared around his body confidently. Likely to make himself appear stronger.

I should know. I had been there once.

"My king," he said as he approached the bottom of the steps. I watched him thoughtfully as he bowed, low and long, before looking me in the eye.

I nodded. A silent gesture of permission to continue speaking.

"My father has grown ill. We—we have no money to pay our tithe. I come here today to offer myself to your court."

My first instinct was to tell the poor boy to go home. But this was the first citizen of this tithe. The first example. So, instead, I looked the boy in the eye and asked, "And why would I want you in my court?"

The boy blinked once. It was his only sign of surprise. "I— I have special gifts, my king. I can fight in your army. I have been gifted with the power of air magic."

"Air magic?"

The boy nodded.

"Show me."

The boy's face lit up, as if he was waiting for this moment all his life. If it were true that he possessed air magic, then maybe he really had.

The boy held his hands out in front of him and closed his eyes for one second before a large gust of wind crossed through the room. Strong enough that I had to stop my crown from falling off my head.

The gust of wind ended just as quickly as it had begun. I instantly stood from my throne.

"How long have you had this magic?" I asked him, genuinely curious to see another fae with magic here in Rewyth.

"The last few months," he answered, keeping his eyes glued to the ground. He was nervous about his power, likely unsure how I would use him. Friend or weapon? Ally or enemy?

"Good," I answered. "We'll have plenty of time to strengthen your gift. You'll live here in the castle and we'll get you the training you need. What is your name, boy?"

The boy's eyes shot up, mouth agape. "Thank you! Thank you! My name is Kylar," he said. "You won't regret this, King Malachi. I promise you!"

I nodded to the guards, and the boy was escorted out of the throne room.

One down. The boy would be useful to us, no doubt.

But I was certain my luck would not continue.

"Bring the next one in," I ordered Ser.

He obeyed, and within a few seconds, I was looking at an older woman. Still fae, but by the looks of it, she was at least a few centuries old.

"I come with your tithe, dear king," she said, tossing a small bag of golden coins at the guard who stood at the bottom of the stairs.

"Your service will not be forgotten," I recited. "The kingdom thanks you."

The woman scoffed and rolled her bright green eyes. "Keep your thanks."

I didn't say another word as she was escorted out of the room.

"What was that about?" I asked the guards as soon as she was gone.

"It's expected to have some resistance to the new reign," one of my guards, Doromir, spoke up. He was an older guard, one that worked for my father for many years.

But he had also worked for me. I trusted him and his

experience. "I can't imagine why someone would resist *my* reign," I muttered. "My father's death was the best thing to happen to this kingdom."

"It's not your reign they resist," he said. "It's change. Who knows what types of rumors have been circulating."

"Great. Let the next one in, then. Wouldn't want to disappoint."

Only it wasn't a citizen who entered the room next.

"What are you doing here?" I asked.

Jade strolled forward, a sleek black dress clinging to her curves as she moved. Her hair was pin-straight down her back, and a golden crown, one that matched my own, sat upon her head.

Saints save me.

"I was informed it was my duty to accompany you at your first tithe. Apologies for my lateness."

I looked for any signs of deception in her face, but found none.

Jade had actually come to run the tithe with me.

The guards watched in awe as she ascended the stone steps, approaching where I sat on the large throne.

"I am your wife, after all," she said when she got close enough.

My eyes flickered down her body, unable to stop themselves from appreciating the pure form of beauty that stood before me.

"Where did you get that crown?" I whispered. Jade watched the way my eyes dragged back up to meet hers, and she smiled.

"Borrowed it from Adeline."

Jade flipped a loose strand of hair over her shoulder and

stepped forward, moving to sit on the armrest of the throne. I didn't pull my arm away as she leaned against me for support. What was she up to? Showing up to a royal event like this on her own free will wasn't something Jade would do.

"Are you sure you're up for this?" I asked her. *Give in now*, I thought. *Give in now, or accept your position as Queen of Rewyth.*

That's what they would see her as. Their queen.

But when Jade's eyes met mine, only inches away, I saw fierce determination.

"Bring it on."

Ignoring the way my stomach flipped, I motioned to Serefin to bring in the next citizen.

It was a fae I recognized. A middle-aged man who had fought in battle with me before. He stormed into the room with such strength that each guard placed their hands on their weapons.

Jade did not budge next to me.

"You kill our true king, yet you sit on his throne and demand I pay money to this wicked kingdom?"

"Careful how you speak to your king," Serefin warned from the back of the room.

The man only grimaced. "He is no king of mine."

From the corner of my eye, I saw Jade's jaw tightened.

"If you are unhappy here, you may leave," I said, choosing each word carefully and calmly.

The man only scoffed. "And go where, exactly?"

"Why should I care?" I replied, letting the coolness of my voice carry through the room. "If you do not wish to pay your tithe like every other citizen because of pure spite, you may leave. Or you will be forced to leave. Choose wisely."

"You would exile me for speaking my opinion regarding the throne?"

The man's presence here alone challenged me. *Clearly.* He was far older than me. He was seasoned. I, however, was not to be messed with. Not after everything I had done for this kingdom. After everything I had done to keep ignorant citizens like *him* safe.

I slowly stood from my throne, taking a step forward before crossing my wrists behind my back. "No," I spoke, much stronger than the last time. "I would exile you for treason. Now pay your tithe and shut your mouth, or gather your things and leave Rewyth for good."

The man shook his head, but after a few moments, he tossed his coin to the guards.

I nodded, not bothering to waste breath on thanking him.

Once the man had left, I returned to Jade at the throne. "See?" she whispered in my ear as I sat. "This is fun."

"I'm glad you're enjoying yourself," I whispered back, barely brushing her ear with my lips before pulling back and facing the doors once more.

I was starting to get bored of citizens entering, tossing coins, and leaving when another familiar face entered.

Another one of my father's men sauntered into the room. *Arthur.*

I stiffened as soon as I saw him. He walked slowly into the room, cocky as ever.

"Well, well, well," he started. "Looks like you got over your father's death quickly."

"Pay your tithe and leave," one of the guards barked.

I held a hand up to silence the guard. "My father's passing was unfortunate, but necessary," I stated.

"Unfortunate, yes," he said. "What's even worse than that tragedy is the *human scum* that sits on your throne."

My power rumbled, but I calmed it quickly. He was trying to get to me. "It was my father's wish to wed me to a human, Arthur. You should be happy to know his intent lives on."

Arthur drew his brows together before sliding his gaze to Jade. I half-expected Jade to flinch away from the fae's attention, but she did no such thing. She didn't move an inch.

"It's a disgrace is what it is," Arthur spat without taking his eyes off Jade. "Tell me, human, why are you here?"

"Don't speak to her," I argued. "You speak to me."

"She is my queen, is she not?"

"It's okay, Mal," Jade whispered to me. "Arthur is free to ask me any question he wishes. To answer," she continued, "I'm here to rule Rewyth beside my husband."

Pride swelled in my chest.

"And what makes you think you are strong enough for that?"

"What makes you think I am not?"

"Any fae in this room could kill you right now," Arthur sneered.

Jade only smiled, calm as ever as she sat perched on the armrest of my throne. "Then do it."

Every guard in the room drew a sword.

Jade did not falter. When Arthur hesitated, she merely raised an eyebrow.

"You heard her," I added when he didn't move. "If you threaten my queen, you better plan on following through."

Jade's blank face flickered with an evil smile.

I fought the urge to reach out and touch her.

Arthur didn't move. He stood at the foot of the steps, clearly confused by Jade's orders.

"Something wrong?" Jade asked. "I'm sitting right here. If you think killing me will be so easy, go right ahead."

Every ounce of my body burned with desire.

Jade stood from her perched position on our throne and stepped toward Arthur. I stayed put, happy to watch as my wife pummeled this man with her power.

I felt it first—a low, magnetic pull of my power to Jade's. She summoned her own magic with a certain authority as she stood before Arthur and grew a large ball of power between her hands.

"Tell me, Arthur," she pushed. "Do you think you could kill me now?"

Arthur stammered in response, unable to form actual words.

Jade stepped forward, cascading down the few stairs that separated her from him.

Her ball of power grew larger. I glanced around the room, and found everyone's eyes glued to Jade in awe.

They felt it, too. The silent buzz of pure strength coming from her.

"What about now?" Jade pushed again. "I'm waiting, Arthur. Go ahead and kill me."

Jade pushed the ball of power forward, just a few paces, but enough to make Arthur stumble backward. He fell on the stone floor but didn't stop scrambling away from Jade's power.

I didn't even try to hide my smile.

Satisfied, Jade released the hold she had on her own magic, causing it to fizzle out.

When she turned to make her way back to me, I recognized the look on her face. It was a look I had rarely seen on her.

Power.

"If you're done insulting my wife now," I said, "you may leave."

But everyone in the room knew that wasn't true. Nobody threatened Jade and escaped with their lives.

Arthur struggled to get to his feet before turning toward the doors.

Although he didn't have time to make it that far.

In one swift motion, my wings lifted me from the throne and cascaded me to block him from exiting.

Horror dripped from every feature on his face when he realized the reality of the situation.

"You picked the wrong side," I growled. His neck snapped like a twig in my hands, and his body fell to the floor.

Nobody looked shocked. The guards in the room quickly got to work disposing of the body while I walked back to the throne.

"Took you long enough," Jade teased as I approached.

I wasn't sure what reaction I expected from her, but it certainly wasn't that. "You're not mad?"

Jade's head spun to me. "Mad?" she asked. "He threatened to kill me! I would have killed him myself if you didn't."

I sat on the throne and placed my hand on Jade's knee. She didn't pull away. "Well, that's good news," I said, "because if anyone else threatens you during this tithe, they'll suffer the same fate."

Jade's mouth tilted upward, only a centimeter, before she returned the cool mask of a queen. "Either by your hands, or by mine."

Her hand came to fall on my shoulder as we signaled for the next citizen to enter.

Perhaps ruling this kingdom wouldn't be as terrible as I had expected.

CHAPTER 16
Jade

I tucked my hair into the back of my jacket. The less identifiable traits I had, the better.

Pulling the fabric over my head only helped slightly. I hoped it would be dark enough in the dungeon to hide my features.

It had worked before.

If I was lucky, this would be the last time.

I placed a hand over my heart, feeling the pounding of every passing second.

The sun had been down for hours now. My feet were silent on the stone floor as I slipped from my bedroom and blended with the shadows in the castle. I became one with them, fluid and dark as I moved toward the dungeon in the path I had taken half a dozen times already.

This time was different, though.

I wasn't leaving alone this time.

I had waited until just after midnight, when the guards rotated positions. This guard in particular, though, had a habit of leaving early to meet with one of the maids in the servants' kitchen.

Terrible habit, that guard.

Goosebumps rose to my skin as I descended further and further into the underground of the castle.

"Sadie," I whispered once I reached her cell, grimacing at the way my voice bounced off the solid dungeon walls. "Where are you?"

"Jade?" her voice in the darkness made me jump. "Jade, what are you doing here?"

"Get up. We're leaving."

I navigated my way over to her, halting when I saw her huddled in the corner.

I closed the distance between us and dropped to my knees next to her. "Sadie, what's wrong? Are you hurt?"

"No," she answered, but her voice was barely a whisper. "No, Jade. I'm not hurt."

I placed my hands on her head. "Saints, Sadie. You're burning up. You're sick."

"I've been through worse."

"We're getting you out of here, Sadie. *Tonight.* You're sick and you can't stay here."

I tried to pull her up by her shoulders, but Sadie didn't budge. "I can't leave, Jade."

"Yes you can. The halls are clear, nobody will notice for days. I have a plan. Let's go."

Sadie took a few shaking breaths and finally met my eyes in the darkness of the dungeons.

"Okay," she said. "But I don't know if I can make it–"

"Put your arm around me," I demanded. "I'll help you walk. It's not far," I lied.

Her skinny arm found mine, and I pulled it over my shoulders.

Sadie was a tall girl, but she felt light as I picked her up from the ground. Too light.

"Ready?" I asked.

"As ready as I'll ever be," she whispered.

And then we were stumbling out of her open cell, down the long corridor of stone toward the entrance of the dungeon.

"I figured I'd find you here," Malachi's voice boomed off the stone.

I froze, Sadie along with me. "We were just–"

"Escaping?"

Even though Malachi was still several feet away, I felt his eyes piercing into me.

I weighed my options. I could try to lie, but Malachi would know it before it even left my mouth. If I told him the truth, I had a slim chance of him taking my side.

He owed me.

Malachi should have known that I stood with him. I showed him that I would defend this kingdom for him.

He needed to trust me on this.

"She's sick, Mal. She can't stay here. She doesn't even deserve to be here in the first place."

"Doesn't deserve to be here?" he repeated. His tone was cold and harsh. A chill ran down my spine.

"No," I said carefully. "She doesn't."

After what happened during the tithe earlier, I knew Malachi expected better from me. Better and worse.

He expected me to be stronger than this.

I had shown Malachi that I was strong. I had shown him I

was on his side. How could I make him see that Sadie was innocent? She was not a threat to me. She never would be.

Malachi's laughter filled the dungeons. "Tell me, Jade. What would you have me do? Let her go free?"

"She had nothing to do with the attack."

"You're too trusting," Malachi spat. "You look at her as an ally because she's a human. If she were fae, would you even blink an eye? Would you care at all?"

I didn't say a word. After the tithe, I knew my behavior shocked Mal. He expected me to stand by his side after all of this. But Sadie was my *friend*. Her breath shallowed beside me.

"Nothing to say now, Jade? No bullshit excuse to why you're helping this human escape? Don't stop there. Why don't I unlock Isaiah's chains for you, too?"

Panic grew in my chest. "Malachi, I–"

"Now that I think about it, that's a great idea. Why don't we all go get your friend *Isaiah*. Let's see what he thinks about you saving his precious friend Sadie. Shall we?"

My blood ran cold.

Malachi pushed past us, barging deep into the dungeons. Leaving us no choice but to stumble after him.

"You need to calm down," I yelled to him. But he was walking much faster than I could carry Sadie. "I was just trying to get Sadie medical treatment. That's it."

"I think you'll need to get a lot more than medical treatment when you see this," he yelled.

Sadie tried to talk, but I quickly shushed her. "Stay quiet. I'll do the talking. He just needs to blow off steam."

"I can hear everything you say," he yelled back. By the

time we rounded the last corner of the dungeon, Sadie nearly fell out of my arms.

Isaiah sat in chains, head hanging down onto his chest. His shirt was gone, and his skin was covered in blood. Some dry, some glistening against the dim lighting.

"Saints, Mal," I mumbled. "Is he–"

"Dead? Unfortunately for him, not yet. I didn't want to end all the fun too soon."

"Why are you doing this?" I asked. "What's the point, Mal? How does this possibly help you?"

"It doesn't help me, Jade. Don't you understand that? He tried to *hurt you*. He nearly got you killed. He nearly got me killed, too. This isn't for helping me, Jade. Isaiah is paying for what he's done."

"What about me?" I asked. My breathing came in short pants. "What about my revenge? What about my justice?" Malachi eyed me carefully. I lifted Sadie's arm off my shoulder and slowly lowered her to the ground before standing again and facing Mal. "What about *me*?"

"What about you, Jade?" he asked. "You want revenge?"

"Yes," I whispered, although it was mostly just a breath. Years of pain, betrayal, and hurt came rushing forward, acknowledging those words as he spoke them. "Yes, I want revenge."

Malachi held his hands out on either side of him. "Then take it," he said, words harsh and blunt. "If you want revenge so badly, Jade, go after it. It's yours."

"I can't," I said, feeling all of those emotions slip away, back to the depths where they belonged. "If I tried getting revenge on everyone who has hurt me, or on everyone who has *tried* to hurt me, I would have nobody left. Nobody."

"You would have me," he added.

"Would I?" My voice cracked, but I didn't care. He needed to hear this. I needed to say it more than anything. "Would I have you, Malachi? After everything we've been through. After everything you've *done.*"

"Yes, Jade!" he barked. Any tenderness from his voice was gone, replaced by the brutal King of Shadows. "Yes, you would have me! Don't you see that? Everything I've done? Dammit, Jade!"

I flinched at his words, but I did not back away.

Not this time.

Not from him.

"*Every single thing* I have done has been for *you*. All of it!"

He stepped forward, close enough now that if I reached out, I would touch him. "And this?" I asked, waving a hand to Isaiah. "Is this also for me?"

"Yes," he responded without a second of hesitation. "It is for you. Because I know you want revenge just as badly as I do, Jade. I can see it in your eyes. Only you can't see it. You can't take Isaiah against his will and chain him up in a dungeon beneath your castle, but I can. *I can!* And I will, Jade. For you, I will."

Sadie whimpered on the ground.

I closed my eyes. Somewhere deep in my soul, into the darkest corners that I had spent years trying to bury, I wanted it. I *delighted* in seeing Isaiah, the man who sold me out, the man who betrayed me, bloody and beaten.

He *did* deserve this.

And I wanted my enemy to suffer.

But Sadie was my friend. Sadie had stood by my side, even if she also stood by Isaiah's.

I opened my eyes and found Sadie in the darkness, attempting to crawl to Isaiah. I walked over and knelt before her, grabbing her chin in my hand.

Something came over me, power I had never felt before. But not from magic.

"Did you know Isaiah was working with Esther to betray us?" I asked her, voice strong.

A single tear fell down her dirty face. "No, I swear it, Jade. I didn't know."

"She's lying," Malachi added from behind us.

Sadie snapped her eyes in his direction, then back at me. "No, Jade! I'm not lying! I'm telling you the truth. I had no idea! He never talked about that stuff with me. He never–"

"You lie!" Malachi yelled this time, his voice echoing off the walls and down the corridor of the underground.

Sadie was fully crying now, tears streaming down her face as she flinched away from Malachi.

And from me.

I stood and turned to Malachi. "She didn't know, Mal," I pushed, not even sure if I could believe the words I was saying.

Malachi shrugged, then closed the distance between himself and Isaiah. "If she didn't know, and if she's truly on our side, then she won't care if I kill her little friend here," he said.

Sadie immediately shot to her feet. "Don't!" she screamed, desperation dripping from her voice. I grabbed her shoulders to push her back, away from Mal and Isaiah. "Don't hurt him!"

"I think we're a little past that by now, don't you, Sadie?"

he whispered. Something in his voice sent a chill down my spine.

I wasn't sure if I hated it or loved it.

"If you really cared about Jade," he continued, "you wouldn't care about a traitor. Would you?"

Malachi pulled a dagger from his belt and cut a thin line across Isaiah's bare chest. It was difficult to even see the cut with the blood already caked over him.

Sadie didn't need to see it, though. To her, it was all the same. She broke down, falling to her knees in the underground once more. "Don't!" she said. "Please don't kill him. He was just trying to protect himself! He didn't mean to get anyone in trouble!" Her words came out in a jumbled mess, drunk with emotion.

Malachi didn't care, though. I didn't expect him to.

Sadie took a long, shaking breath and looked Malachi directly in the face. "Please," she whispered. "Show him mercy."

"You want mercy?" he repeated. I stayed still where I stood, not daring to move an inch.

Not wanting to stop the scene before me.

Those dark shadows deep within me whispered for *more*.

"There is only one mercy for a man like Isaiah. For a traitor. For a man who tried to kill my *wife*."

My heart pounded in my chest. I knew what was coming.

Malachi was the King of Shadows.

Death would be a gift to Isaiah.

As if he read my thoughts, Malachi grabbed Isaiah's head with both hands and, in the blink of an eye, snapped his neck.

Sadie screamed.

Isaiah's chains kept him from falling sideways to the ground.

I stood there, not able to look away. A numbness I recognized all too well spread through my chest, across my entire body.

Isaiah was dead. Isaiah betrayed me, he betrayed Malachi, and now he was dead.

Malachi killed him.

I looked at Malachi, who was already staring at me.

Waiting for my reaction.

Did he want me to hate him? Did he want me to run away? Or did he think I would sink to the floor like Sadie, screaming my lungs out at the horror?

I did none of those things. I wasn't afraid of Malachi. I wasn't afraid of the things he did.

To be honest, I hated that I wasn't disgusted by him. No, I was the furthest thing from disgusted.

I saw something in him that I recognized deeply within myself. The horror. The shame. The guilt. The power.

I wanted it all.

"Let her go," I demanded. "She's gone through enough."

Malachi swallowed once. "Fine," he said. "Now she knows what will happen if she crosses us in the future. Run into the woods and find your way back to Fearford. You are not welcome back here, Sadie. Let this be a reminder to you of what will happen if you betray Jade."

My stomach twisted at the way Sadie scraped herself off the floor and stumbled to Isaiah, checking to make sure he was really dead.

He was.

"Go, Sadie," I said. I kept my eyes on Malachi. I couldn't

look at her. Not now. Not after this. "Go before he changes his mind."

Sadie was sobbing hysterically, but she understood. She knew this was her only chance.

She pushed past Malachi and I, sobbing with every weak step, and she was gone.

"You didn't have to do that in front of her," I hissed. "She loved him."

Malachi shook his head. "She didn't love him," he muttered. "And she'll get over it."

"You're unbelievable," I said. "You drag us back here for what? This abusive show of power?"

Malachi stomped forward, inches from my face. "How do you think I felt, Jade, when I saw you escaping with her? You're supposed to be on my side. After the tithe, I thought we were on the same page. What was I supposed to do? Let you both go?"

"Nothing! You were supposed to do nothing! I was helping a friend. You would have done the same."

"No!" he yelled back. "No, I wouldn't have!" He stepped forward again, and this time, I took a step back, pressing my back to the cold stone behind me.

"You could have shown him mercy. For her sake."

Malachi placed his arm on the stone behind me, pinning me to the wall with his own body. "No, I couldn't have. You know that just as well as I do. He deserved to die. You know that."

"And you're the one that decides that?"

"I am the King."

"The King of Shadows," I repeated.

Malachi smiled, wicked and beautiful. "Yes, Jade," he

whispered. His breath tickled my cheek. "I am the King of Shadows. My enemies will die merciless deaths at my hands. My allies will know no defeat when they fight by my side. You, of all people, should realize that."

"As your wife?" I asked.

He stared at me a second longer before answering, "As my queen."

CHAPTER 17
Malachi

"This is required?" I asked Serefin. He was the only guard I allowed in my rooms these days. I trusted the others enough, but time would tell whether or not they were truly loyal to me.

The dinner of celebration to formally announce my new reign as King of Rewyth was set to take place tonight. It was more of a formality than anything, but Saints, it was going to be a pain in my ass.

"Unfortunately, yes. But you are the King. I suppose you can make your own rules now."

I shook my head and strapped my belt around my waist, making sure each weapon was secured tightly in its spot.

"Hours of bullshit conversations with people I don't even like."

"The court members were chosen by your father," Serefin reminded me. "But that doesn't mean they can't be replaced. Hear them out, but determine your own future."

I considered his words. The court members were going to fight every single thing I said tonight. I knew that. They had been loyal to my father, but their greed controlled them more than loyalty.

If I played my cards right, I would have no problem winning them over.

The court members were composed of fae that had been around much longer than I had. Some of them grew up with my father. Others were new. Each one held a great amount of land, money, or something else that had been deemed beneficial to Rewyth.

And because of that, each one of them thought they had a voice in this court. In the decisions made here.

What a joke.

"Jade will be there?" I asked Ser, keeping my voice calm.

He nodded. "Adeline is with her. They're getting ready as we speak."

"Good," I muttered. "Perhaps she'll distract everyone from stupid court politics."

Serefin laughed. "Careful what you wish for, brother. I'm sure half the kingdom has heard of the prophecy by now. Not to mention her special abilities."

Saints.

Jade could protect herself. There was no doubt that someone tonight was going to say something offensive to her. Someone would try to make a smart-ass comment about her place in this kingdom, her place as my wife.

Her place as queen.

And I had no doubt that if Jade didn't shut them up, I would.

Anyone who disrespected Jade disrespected *me*, in turn.

I had to admit, I was curious to see who would be bold enough to try.

But it was true. Jade *did* have a special ability. Certainly, rumors had spread by now, especially after her show of power at the tithe.

I was prepared to fight anyone who challenged her magic.

Was Jade?

I turned to the door and clapped Serefin on the arm. "I guess there is no better time than right now," I said. "Let's get this over with."

Serefin opened my bedroom door and stepped aside.

Only when I stepped into the hallway, I wasn't alone.

At the opposite end of the hall, Jade did the same.

Adeline had dressed her in a low-cut corset gown with a large skirt that moved with each step she took.

Even from far away, she looked stunning.

She would be the talk of the dinner tonight. No doubt about that.

"Good luck with that, brother," Serefin whispered to me. I walked down the hall, closing the distance between us, and held my arm out to Jade. After what happened in the dungeons last night, I wasn't sure she would accept.

I didn't regret it. Not for a second. Jade had to see who I really was. She needed to see, deep down, what I would sacrifice for her. *Who* I would sacrifice for her. Because nothing else mattered when she was around. Nothing else mattered, except that she was okay. Anyone who threatened that would pay.

Sadie had left—I made sure of it from a distance after Jade stormed away. What Jade didn't understand, though, was that I *had* shown mercy. I *had* shown Sadie mercy. I had sure as shit shown Isaiah mercy by killing him swiftly after dragging his poor life out for weeks in the dungeons.

He had given me everything I needed.

I was half tempted to rush to Jade and tell her that it wasn't personal, or that I wasn't myself. But neither of those things were true. It was personal on a deep, soul-aching level that I couldn't even understand myself. It was personal enough that I was willing to rip the head off any man who touched her. No matter what they were to me.

It was personal enough that I couldn't think straight around her. I could no longer see the big picture when she was near.

But the way I acted last night *was* myself. I hadn't felt that free in a long, long time. For weeks now, I had been restricting myself. Hiding myself. Trying to fit into the perfect version of me that Jade might actually understand.

Everything was clear to me, now. Jade did understand. I saw it in the sparkle of her eye last night, as she watched me snap Isaiah's neck without a single blink. When Sadie had dropped to the ground in screams, Jade stared at me.

Jade stared into me, deep into the dark corner that never saw light.

She saw it all.

And she did not look away.

"Are you ready?" I asked Jade as I held my arm out to her. She took it gently, delicately touching my bicep with her small palm.

"No," she answered, keeping her head straight ahead. Serefin and Adeline fell into step behind us. "I'm not. I'm not going to pretend like this kingdom appreciates a human as their queen, even if I do have special gifts."

My mouth twitched before I could control it.

"What?" she asked. "You think that's funny?"

"No," I said. "It's just nice to hear you calling yourself queen."

Jade's cheeks flushed red, and she snapped her attention back to the hallway ahead of us. "I don't see myself getting out of it easily."

"So you've decided to accept it?"

"I suppose I have," she said. "Because I'm being thrown into this world either way, right?"

Part of me wanted to open these doors and let her run far, far away from everything. The prophecy, my mother, her own family. She deserved better. She deserved a fresh start.

But that wasn't possible.

The other part of me knew that, and didn't want her out of my sight for a single second. Selfishly, I was glad she was here. I was glad she was in this castle. Every time I pictured this life without her, the vast void of loneliness staring me directly in the face became too much. Too heavy.

But with Jade, everything was…better.

"It will be over before you know it. I'll formally announce my new reign, we'll eat until we're sick, and then we'll be waltzing out of there like it never even happened."

Jade sighed as we turned a corner, the massive dining hall doors coming into view. I felt her tense up on my arm. "We're never that lucky, and you know it."

I wanted to tell her she was wrong, but I knew she wasn't. Luck didn't have a way of finding us.

But we made our own.

A guard near the door stepped forward and announced our arrival. I heard the scratching of chairs on the wooden floor as everyone stood from their seats, anticipating our arrival.

"Showtime, my queen," I whispered.

And we entered the dining hall.

Jade tried to pull away from my arm, but I quickly caught her hand and tugged lightly, letting her know she wasn't going anywhere. We were one unit now.

The truth was, we always had been.

"Thank you for coming," I said to the room. "Please, be seated."

I walked to the head of the table, taking Jade along with me, and we sat in the two open chairs. After Serefin and Adeline sat on either side of us, the table was filled.

The faces around me were mostly friendly. My brothers sat nearby, along with court members. Many were the same court members that watched as Jade was tormented under my father's reign. A few I didn't recognize sat near the end of the table.

And their faces weren't welcoming.

It was going to be a long night, indeed.

Jade sat in her seat, but I could practically feel the tension rising off her.

"Let me start this celebratory evening off by announcing that the deadlings who attacked us the other night were killed. Every single one. Not one of those beasts left alive."

A few nods of approval, but that was it.

I continued. "I also want to say that it was not a random attack. Based on what we know, we believe it was a warning."

Cue the muttering and whispering around the table.

"A warning?" Adonis spoke up. "A warning from who? For what?"

Wine. I definitely needed wine.

I picked up the cup in front of me and took a long gulp.

"The Paragon has their eye on us. However, they aren't our only enemy. It's possible it could have come from elsewhere, but odds are, the Paragon sent those beasts our way to try and shake us up."

"Why would they do that? Why would they want that?"

I looked over to Jade, who was already staring at me, jaw set.

"Because Jade has the power that they want. They'll come after her. Sooner or later, they'll come."

"And what is she to us?" one of the strangers at the end of the table asked. "Why should we protect her?"

I had to remind myself that we were in public. Everyone at this table had their eyes glued on me.

But didn't that make this a perfect time to put everyone in their place?

Jade wasn't only my wife. She was now the *Queen of Rewyth*. It was time they treated her–and spoke about her–as such.

"Jade is the peacemaker, spoken of in hundreds of old prophecies. My mother recently told me that–"

"Your mother?" one of the men chimed in. "She's alive?"

I silently cursed to myself for not bringing this up earlier. A handful of people knew that my mother—the true Queen of Rewyth—still lived. Even fewer people knew that she had betrayed me.

And she was hiding away in the dungeons of our castle. That was something only Serefin, my brothers, and I knew.

"My mother is not the topic of this dinner," I yelled. My voice was strong enough that the delicate plates on the table rattled. "We're here to discuss my reign moving forward, and the challenges we'll be facing in the coming weeks. If anyone has a problem with that, you can leave now."

Nobody moved.

"And if anybody has a problem with our stance on protecting our queen—my wife, then speak up now."

Again, nobody moved.

But I doubted that would be the last I heard of it.

"Good. Now we can move on to discussing—" my attention stalled on a familiar fae at the end of the table.

Kara.

"What are you doing in here? This is for court members only," I stated. I felt Jade stiffen next to me.

She looked genuinely shocked. "Oh," she placed a dramatic hand on her chest. "You haven't heard? My father has chosen me to stand in his place in court."

"No," I barked. "That's not happening."

"But you can't–"

I slammed my hands on the wooden table and let my black wings flare out either side of me. "Please, Kara," I said, "continue arguing with your king."

My brothers choked on their laughter.

"She has a right to be here, King Malachi," one of the other court members chimed in. He was older, but I couldn't quite remember his name.

"Nobody has a right to be here," I half-yelled to the table. I reached over and clasped Jade's hand. "This is my kingdom now. I understand that things were run a certain way when my father sat in this chair, but he's gone. He was corrupt and vile and greedy. He was lost. And his reign will *not* continue. So when I say that a court member goes, he or she goes. Understand, Kara?"

I turned my attention back to her.

For once, she actually looked shocked.

Her eyes slid over to Jade, just for a second, before she stood from her seat and strutted out of the room.

"Good," I said again. "Let me remind you all that traitors are not welcome here. Anyone who questions me can leave. Anyone who questions Jade can leave. Understood?"

"With all due respect," the same man spoke, "your mother was the true queen. As your father's first wife, she holds certain rights here. If she is still alive and willing to accept the position, the throne is rightfully hers."

I was prepared for this topic to arise. Historically, it was rare for a woman to sit on the throne. Rewyth, however, held this unique tradition.

But it had been decades since my mother had been seen in Rewyth. Most of the kingdom will have forgotten about her presence here. And most of the kingdom would prefer a male on the throne, anyway.

My argument was strong.

I paused. "My mother is nothing. She is a traitor, she is a selfish witch, and she is no longer a free member of this kingdom."

"Why?"

Lucien leaned across the table and answered before I could. "Why?" he repeated. "You question your own king? Esther is nothing more than an old woman who wants to cheat her way out of consequences. Believe Malachi when he says she is a traitor."

The man clenched his jaw and leaned back in his chair. He had heard enough.

"Now about the prophecy," I started. "Jade's life is at risk every single day. The prophecy names her as the peacemaker. As you all know, the Paragon is in place to keep the power between witches and fae equal. Well, Jade's power will change all of that. Whichever side uses her power in the curse-breaking ritual will have access to her power. Will have control of all power. The Paragon is coming for her to use her power for themselves."

"And why is that so bad? They are fair, King Malachi. The Paragon will know what to do with her."

I wanted to yell into his face. No, they were not fair. These fae were only fed spoonfuls of information to make themselves believe as much.

"It is bad because they will kill Jade for it. And as Jade is my wife, I'm sure you can see how I'm not letting that happen."

The man glanced at Jade, then nodded.

Jade's hand tightened slightly in mine.

Serefin spoke next. "Have we heard back from the scouts? Any movement on the horizons?"

Adonis answered, "I haven't heard a single thing. It's silent out there."

"They're waiting until we drop our guard," I added. "They will hit us hard, and it will be soon."

Another man at the end of the table leaned in and asked, "Do we even have the resources to fight them? If they come for our queen, how will we defend her?"

Our queen. A wave of relief washed over me to hear those words from a court member.

And it was immediately ripped away when the man to his right began laughing.

I recognized him. He was one of the men who held me back while Jade was whipped.

My vision blurred. "Something funny?"

He stopped laughing long enough to answer, "You kill your father, you remove a court member, you hide our true queen, and you deplete the castle's resources in the name of a human. Yet you call *us* traitors?"

It took one second for my power to unleash upon him. He fell out of his chair, doubling over on the ground in pain.

Others gasped in surprise. I only narrowed my focus. More pain. More torture.

It only lasted ten seconds or so, but to him, it would feel like hours.

When I pulled my power back, he was nothing more than an empty threat on the ground.

"Yet another one of my father's men that cannot see our new way. Please, excuse yourself from this room."

He couldn't walk, though. Two guards from the door dragged him out.

I knew my father's remaining men would be the ones to threaten me.

I came ready to tear them all down.

Jade stood from her chair, the wooden pegs scratching the floor as she shoved it backward. "The Paragon will come," she repeated. Her voice was so strong, it echoed off the stone walls around us. "They want to use me for my power and kill me. You don't know me. You have no reason to believe in me. But I will tell you this..." She glanced at me before continuing, a sparkle of life twinkling in her eye. "If you stand by me—if you are willing to fight for me in the face of the Paragon—I will stop at nothing to make this the most powerful kingdom in history. How would you all feel to have a power like Malachi's? Like my own?"

The others said nothing, but I knew she had hit a soft spot. I saw the longing in their eyes.

They were men. Of course, they wanted power.

"Then it seems we are on the same page," I added. "Let's eat."

CHAPTER 18

Jade

I ate until I was sure the stitching on my corset would burst open. After the initial discussion, nobody seemed to question what I was doing in court. For the most part, a few suspicious glances were the only sign of questioning coming from the other members.

Malachi explained the process of the sacrifice and the details of what the Paragon wanted to do with me. It took a while to convince everyone of the prophecy, but once Malachi had explained it fully, they didn't question it. I wasn't sure they were willing to jump in front of an arrow for me, but at least they were listening.

That was a start.

We stayed there for hours. Discussions of politics turned into old memories of battle and war. Bickering turned to friends reliving decades of life together.

Malachi leaned across the table, arguing to Eli about who could shoot an arrow further.

I took the moment to sneak away, out of the dwindling crowd of the ballroom and into the halls of the castle.

Somehow, the night had actually been enjoyable. Watching Malachi command the room as King of Rewyth warmed a place in my soul that I didn't know had chilled over.

I walked through the dark castle, turning the hall to my bedroom.

"Miss me?" a voice rang out in the darkness.

I spun around to find Kara walking toward me. "Not really, no. Although by the looks of you stalking me, it seems as though you certainly missed me."

"That's too bad," she spat. "Because I've been waiting to see you again. I wasn't so sure I ever would after you left the first time."

"You mean after you conspired with Esther to kill me?"

She only shrugged. I never found out how much she actually knew about Malachi's brothers working with Esther, but Kara meant nothing to me. She was an annoying fly that needed to get out of my way.

I turned to walk away from her, but she was in front of me in an instant. Even as a woman, her fae speed was shocking.

"What do you want, Kara?"

She smiled. "The peacemaker, huh?" she teased. "It must feel nice knowing you're not just a stupid little human anymore."

I tried to push past her. She blocked me.

"Trust me," I warned her. "You don't want to do this. And I'm not just a peacemaker, I'm your queen, in case you forgot."

A growl of anger escaped her, and before I knew what was happening, she had me pinned to the wall.

My power flared.

"Malachi might think you're special," she hissed, "but you will never be anything more than human scum."

My power flared again, and I didn't fight it this time. A burst of light flashed through the dark hallway.

Kara screamed.

When I opened my eyes, she was cowering away on the floor, crawling backward.

I knelt next to her. "Next time you threaten me," I whispered in her ear, "I'll kill you."

CHAPTER 19

Jade

"It's beautiful," Tessa whispered, staring in awe at the gorgeous greenery around us. I knew she would like it here. The lagoon had a certain presence of peace that instantly made us feel calm.

I still remembered the first time Adeline brought me here. I thought the exact same thing. Rewyth wasn't this nasty, criminal hole in the dirt like we all wanted it to be.

Rewyth was beautiful. Nature flowed in and out like breath. I looked around us, admiring all of the changes that had grown and bloomed since I had last been here.

One could spend days in this lagoon and still not appreciate its beauty in entirety.

"It is, isn't it?" I asked.

"You said you saw a...a..."

"Tiger," I finished for her. "And I didn't just see one. It attacked me while I was swimming right here in the lagoon."

Tessa stared at me, eyes wide, like I was the most interesting person alive. She used to look at me with that same look when we were younger. She used to look at me like I was...*special*. Like I meant something to her.

I missed that look.

"I was fine after Malachi stepped in," I added, "besides the nasty cut on my leg."

I lifted up my leg to show her the scar.

"Saints," she mumbled.

I smacked her arm lightly. "Hey! Who said you could start saying things like that?"

"Please," she added, turning back to look into the deep blue lagoon. "I spend my days with father. I hear more cursing than the insides of a tavern."

It was a joke; I knew it was. Yet still, something deep in my chest twisted.

Tessa was my baby sister. She wasn't supposed to experience this harshness.

I did that so she didn't have to. I took on all of that so she didn't have to.

Tessa sat on the ground, dangling her feet into the blue water of the lagoon. "So...I guess it's really not so bad here."

"No," I added, sitting next to her and dipping my own bare feet into the cool water. "I guess it's not."

"You seem happier," she said without looking at me.

What was I supposed to say to that? *Was* I happier? I was nothing when I lived at home. I was Tessa's provider, and I was the beating bag when my father came home drunk, but I had no future. No prospects. No life.

Here? I had a target on my back. I was married—against my will—to a king, which now made me a queen in a kingdom full of people who probably didn't give a shit if I was dead or alive.

But still. I found myself waking up every morning with a purpose. I found myself laughing, even when the dark parts of my soul told me I would never laugh again.

I found myself having hope. Which scared me more than any threat from the Paragon.

"It's...complicated," I explained.

"You can tell me, you know," she added. "I know you were the one taking care of me all those years at home, Jade. I never knew exactly how much you did for me, but I know now. I do. And I never actually thanked you for all you did."

"You don't need to thank me."

"I do, Jade. Because you didn't ask for this."

I suddenly felt the urge to throw up. No, I didn't ask for this. Not a damn thing. But I wasn't going to let Tessa take a beating from our father. I wasn't going to let her starve.

I wasn't going to let anyone who supported me get hurt.

Malachi, Adeline, Tessa. They were all my family now.

I may have gone through the deepest pits of darkness over the last few months, but I found myself with more to lose than ever before.

"I think...I think if things were different, I might actually be happy here," I admitted. *Shit. Did I really just say that to her?*

Tessa looked at me, eyes glazed over. "Me too," she added, which surprised me more than anything.

Footsteps crunched on the forest floor behind us. I tensed immediately, grabbing Tessa's arm. Adeline said this place was sacred, practically special just for her. Who else would be coming here?

"Look what we have here," a small group of fae, maybe

five, approached from the brush. "Our queen and her baby sister. How sweet."

"Leave us alone," I demanded.

The fae in front, a young male by the looks of it, stopped dead in his tracks with a dramatic wave of his hands to stop the fae that walked behind him.

"Watch out," he teased. "Our queen is giving us an order. It wouldn't be polite to disobey."

Tessa tried to whisper something in my ear but I quickly shushed her.

"Stand up and get behind me," I whispered.

She did as I ordered, and the two of us stood up against the group of fae.

"What are you doing here?" I asked them, trying to make my voice as strong as possible. "What do you want?"

The leader of the group looked around and scanned the men behind him. Something about the way they looked at each other made the hair on the back of my neck stand up. "We hear you have power, human," he started. "We want to see it."

"What?" I instinctively reached back and gripped Tessa. I wasn't letting these bastards touch her.

The fae stepped forward. There were now just a few feet between us. "I said I want to see your power, human. Unless, of course, it's all fake."

"Fake? Why would I lie about having power? How would...that's ridiculous."

The fae took another step forward. I debated calling out for help, but there would be nobody around here. Everyone was inside the castle. "I don't care what it is," he said. "I just want to see it. Prove to us that you're special. You are our queen, after all."

"I don't have to prove anything to you. Alarms began shouting at me in my mind. This was bad. This was trouble.

Tessa tensed behind me. I couldn't back up anymore without pushing her into the lagoon.

"You're not *afraid*, are you?" the fae asked, taking yet another step forward.

Yes, I was afraid. Not for myself, but for Tessa.

She was brand new to this world, thrown in against her will just like I had been. She didn't need this trouble. She didn't ask for it.

"Back up," I barked, shocked at the boldness in my voice.

This only elicited a short burst of laughter from the fae and his posse.

"Malachi won't like hearing about this," I added. I hated that I had to resort to Malachi as a threat, but I'll be damned if I was going to let anyone mess with my sister. I would set my pride aside for this.

But the fae didn't even blink. "It doesn't look like your big, bad husband is anywhere in sight, now does it?" he asked.

Another step forward.

My blood was hot in my veins, beating loud in my ears.

I couldn't use my magic. Not now. Not with Tessa so close. If I hurt her...

And that was if I was even capable of wielding it right now with so much pressure.

If I lost control, I could kill us all.

"Do we have a problem here?" another voice asked from the tree line. I snapped my attention to the figure who stepped into the light.

Adonis.

I could have dropped to the ground with relief.

The fae in front of me backed up immediately, as did the few behind him.

"No problem," he lied. "We were just introducing ourselves to our queen. That's all."

Adonis eyed me, and I watched as his eyes flickered quickly to the tight grip I had on Tessa.

"Right," Adonis sneered, stepping forward. He seemed as calm as ever, arms lazily crossed behind his back and shoulders relaxed. "And I'm sure my brother won't appreciate hearing about this, either."

The fae mumbled a slur of words I couldn't understand.

Adonis took another step forward. "If you approach her again, it won't be me you answer to. Understand?"

"Bastard," one of the fae in the back of the group mumbled.

I tightened my grip on Tessa once more.

Adonis only laughed, low and cruel, before drawing the sword from his belt.

Tessa squealed behind me.

"Care to say that to my face?" Adonis asked.

"Five against one?" the fae in front started. "Your odds are low, Adonis. We meant no trouble."

Bullshit.

"I'll take those odds," Adonis sneered, pulling his sword into position between them.

My heart raced in my chest. I knew what I needed to do. I was the queen. I was the peacemaker. I was powerful.

I was no longer the helpless girl begging for her life.

No, I would never be that girl again.

I felt the rush of power in my body, the same way I had felt it in the dungeon with Esther. The same way I had felt it at the tithe.

I could do this. I could show them how powerful I was.

I slowly let go of Tessa, so slowly that nobody would notice, and I took a tiny step forward.

The group of fae now each had a weapon drawn, although it was clear that none of them had as extensive training as Adonis.

I stepped slowly to Adonis's side.

And I held my hands out in front of me.

"Jade," he warned, but I caught the slight hint of intrigue in his voice. He wanted me to do this, too.

I let my anger become tangible, focusing on that need for power that fueled me deep inside my soul.

I wanted them to pay. I wanted them all to pay. I could protect my own, now. I didn't need Adonis or anyone else coming to my rescue.

Before I could stop myself, my body became a rush of fire, anger, desperation, and power. A flash of light snapped before me, and I heard Tessa scream somewhere in the back of my mind.

It was a release, a release of the helplessness I was feeling, of the desperation, the embarrassment, the need for power.

I took a deep breath and opened my eyes.

The fae who had been antagonizing me was on the ground, unconscious.

I staggered backward, bumping into Adonis.

"Get out of here," he growled. "Take your sister and go."

He was lifeless, unmoving. A layer of burnt skin covered the majority of his front side. "Did I..."

"I don't know," Adonis snapped. "But you need to go. Find Malachi."

The power that I had felt seconds ago was replaced with something else, something much darker. My stomach dropped, my entire body shook with the question.

Had I killed him?

Had I killed a fae?

Tessa grabbed my hand and pulled me toward the direction of the brush, snapping me out of my trance. "We have to go, Jade," she whispered. "Come on."

I let her lead me away, but I didn't miss the desperate screams for help that came from the fae who stayed behind. And I didn't miss the way Adonis threatened them all to stay quiet about it.

He was dead. He had to be.

Nobody looked like that and survived. Not even a fae.

"Tessa, I–"

"Stop," she interrupted with a voice I had never heard her use before. "Stop whatever you're about to say. You could have just saved our lives back there, Jade."

"Is he dead?" I whispered, as if Tessa would know the answer.

She stopped walking and turned to face me, gripping me so tightly on the shoulders that pain shot down my arms. "Who cares if he's dead, Jade? He was going to hurt us!"

"I didn't mean to," I whispered. My voice cracked. "I didn't mean to hurt him, Tessa. I just wanted him to leave us alone."

"I know," she said. She let go of my arms and pulled me into a hug.

Saints, she was nearly as tall as I was. When did she get so tall?

When she pulled away, she had a small smile on her face.

"What?" I asked. What could she possibly be smiling about? Did she understand that I had just killed someone?

"You really are magic. I've heard the rumors, but I didn't believe them. I mean, our whole lives, and we didn't know!"

"I know," I responded, suddenly feeling a wave of guilt.

What I would give to go back to that naive version of us.

That version of us that only had to worry about finding food and staying away from our drunk father.

Now? The list of things to worry about never ended.

"Jade, wait up!" Adonis yelled as he caught up to us.

Tessa immediately stiffened again, taking a slight step to stand behind me.

"What do you want?" I asked.

"He's alive," Adonis said. "Barely."

I exhaled a deep breath, and my shoulders finally dropped from their tight position.

"Saints," I mumbled. "Are they pissed?"

"Don't worry about them. I let them know that was a merciful punishment for antagonizing their queen and her sister."

Okay. We were going to be okay.

"Thank you, Adonis. If you hadn't showed up..."

"You would have kicked all of their asses, I'm sure of it." I hadn't really noticed the bright green specks in Adonis's eyes before. He was nothing like Malachi, but in his own ways, he wasn't hideous. I supposed I had never really looked at him before. But now, standing before me after practically saving my life, I saw him.

"Tessa and I appreciate it," I added.

Tessa finally stepped out from behind me and looked at Adonis herself.

Adonis looked at her, too.

"Hello," he said, extending his hand. "It's nice to officially meet you, little Farrow."

Tessa took another step forward, and I watched the way her eyes flickered to his silver wings. "Hello," she said back to him, placing her tiny hand in his.

He shook it respectfully.

Saints, I must have been dreaming. Because I never would have imagined this type of interaction between either of them.

"Let's get you two back to the castle," Adonis said after dropping Tessa's hand. "I would suggest that we don't tell your husband about this, but…"

"He'll find out anyway," I finished for him. "I'll tell him. He'll take it better coming from me."

Adonis nodded in agreement, and we made our way back to the castle.

To find Malachi.

CHAPTER 20
Malachi

"**Y**ou did *what?*"

Jade took a long, shaking breath, and began explaining once more. "I had no choice," she said, stammering and trying to breathe through her words. "I tried to control it, Mal, I swear I tried to keep it under control."

Saints, did she really think I was mad at her for using her power? Did she not understand how absolutely sexy that was?

"Jade," I said, stepping forward and grabbing her chin, forcing her to look me in the eye. "Take a deep breath."

Jade had come straight to my room to tell me. Adonis had left to walk Tessa back to her room, leaving Jade to explain the entire thing.

Jade took a long, shaking breath under my touch. "Good. Now take another one." She did. "I'm not angry," I said. "And you did nothing wrong."

She looked at me with glossy eyes. "I almost killed them, Mal. I could have killed them all!"

"But you didn't."

"But I could have!"

"Listen to me, Jade. If anyone so much as looks at you the wrong way, they should expect nothing less than death. Do you understand that?" Jade blinked, but didn't say another word. "And if I would have seen that, I would have killed them all myself. Not a single one of them would have survived for what they were about to do to you."

Jade shook her head, taking her chin out of my grip. "You don't even know what they were going to do."

"I don't care," I explained. "They wanted to see you weak. They disrespect you by challenging you, Jade, and in turn, they disrespect me. And I won't tolerate either of those things in this castle."

Jade walked over and sat on the edge of my bed. It had been so long since she had slept in this room with me, it stirred something deep inside me just seeing her sitting there.

"What if I never learn to control it?"

"You will."

"How do you know that?"

I walked over and sat next to her, keeping a safe distance between us. "Because I've been exactly where you are, Jade. I know exactly what you're feeling right now."

"Yeah, right," she scoffed. "You don't go around losing control often."

"Not anymore, but it took me decades to get here. I've lost sleep over the things I've done, Jade. I've killed hundreds of innocent people, and that wasn't all on purpose."

She finally looked at me with eyes wide. "Really?"

I nodded. "When I first discovered my power, I was a nightmare. My father practically locked me up so I would quit hurting people. It flared anytime I was angry, which, if you can imagine, was very often."

She smiled, but it didn't reach her eyes. "You don't seem to have that problem anymore," she noted.

"No. I don't."

"How many people will I kill before I learn?" she asked.

Her doe eyes were still watery, and I had to fight the urge to reach out and comfort her. "I don't know." It was an honest answer.

"I don't want to be a monster, Mal, but.."

"But?"

"But there was something about feeling that power that felt so...good. I felt powerful, Mal. They wanted to push me around and I..."

"And you stopped them."

"Yes. I stopped them. But if I would have killed him..."

"What?" I asked, pushing her even though I knew I should stop. "What would have been so bad about killing someone who wanted to hurt you?"

Jade shook her head and rubbed her hands down her face. "That's the thing, Mal. I don't know if I would have hated it...because as soon as I saw what I did, deep down, there was a small part of me somewhere that actually hoped he was dead."

I hid my smile. Jade was more like me than I had originally thought.

It's not that I wanted to kill people. Truly, I didn't. But there was something about possessing a power so strong, any enemy could be shoved to their knees before you.

It felt powerful, yes. But it felt *right*. It felt like it belonged to me. All those times where I was helpless, all those times where I could do nothing but stand and watch as my father did what he pleased.

Even though I was the King of Shadows.

No, I would never be that helpless again.

I had this power for a reason. The Saints had given it to me for a purpose, and I wasn't just going to stand by and watch injustice continue.

Yes, I killed people. Many people. Some good, some bad.

But at the end of the day, my enemies quit breathing. And that's what mattered. That's why my power rumbled in my blood.

I saw it in Jade's eyes, too. The need to right the wrongs. The need for justice. And in turn, the need for power.

"It's okay, Jade," I assured her. "There's nothing wrong with hoping your enemies are dead."

"But they were members of this kingdom. That does not make them *my* enemies."

"No?" I teased. "Because at one point, I think it sure did."

A flash of amusement flickered across her face. "I liked using my power," she said after some time. "And that scares me."

I ignored the voice in my head that screamed at me not to do this, and I slid my body closer to Jade's on the bed, grabbing hold of her arm so she looked me in the eye once more.

"Being powerful shouldn't scare you," I whispered. "It should excite you. You were made for this, Jade. I knew that the moment I saw you."

"I don't want to become like...like everyone else who put me down. Who abused their power. I don't want to be like them."

"Then don't," I said. "Become the advocate. Become the one that shows up when nobody else does. I don't know what you are, Jade, but as far as I'm concerned, you're still human. You can be *their* power. You can be *their* voice."

"The humans will never accept me again," she stated coldly. "Especially after everything that's happened."

"You don't know that," I said. "They'll love having you, Jade, because you're on their side."

"Am I?" she asked. She stood and began pacing again, this time lost in her own mind. "Am I really on their side?"

I asked her a simple question. "You're on my side, aren't you?"

Jade stopped pacing and looked at me. "I am."

I closed the distance between us, close enough that if she even took a deep breath, her chest would touch mine.

The space that lingered between us was a silent question.

"Are you with me in this, Jade?"

I could feel her emotional turmoil. Her power reacted to it, causing mine to do the same.

Jade tilted her head to meet my eyes. "I'm with you, Malachi."

"Be their queen," I pushed. "Be powerful and fearless and wild. And be *mine*."

Jade took the last step and pressed her body against mine. My power flared in reaction. Hers did, too. A small tendril of light surrounded her body.

I wasn't afraid of it, though.

Jade couldn't hurt me. I couldn't hurt her. We were made for each other.

She must have realized this, too, because her small hands found their way to my back, pulling me even closer.

"I am yours, Malachi Weyland."

CHAPTER 21

Jade

I had never been more sure of anything in my entire life.

Malachi kissed me slowly, taking his time as he tasted my lips, my neck, my collarbone. His hands wandered my body and his skin created a trail of fire everywhere he touched.

Kissing him didn't feel like it had before. Malachi didn't feel like the evil fae prince who had to be gentle with this human wife. No, Malachi felt like my equal.

He *was* my equal.

I could feel my own magic rolling in excitement as I kissed him back, pushing against his body and guiding him to the bed. He let me lead him, giving me control and surrendering to my touch.

He was no longer in control of me. He was no longer the only powerful one.

Malachi was my equal in more ways than one. Our kisses grew fiercer, I grew hungrier and hungrier for more of him.

More of my match.

More of my husband.

Malachi leaned back onto the bed and pulled me on top of him. "I love you, Jade. I had no idea how much I needed you."

I kissed him again. "No more than I needed you," I replied.

How true those words were.

Malachi tucked his wings in and rolled us over, covering my body with his as he continued to devour my body with his hands.

I closed my eyes and let the euphoria of his touch spread over me.

I needed this for too long. I *wanted* this for too long.

Malachi's lips were hot against my neck as he pulled the shoulder of my top down, exposing more of the skin there.

It wasn't enough. I wanted to be closer to him. I wanted us to become one.

To finally be what I felt in my soul we should have been all along.

Malachi sensed this, too. His eyes locked to mine as he pulled back, just enough to slide his hands under my tunic. He paused, only for a moment, waiting for my approval.

Instead of answering with words, I pulled the rest of it up and over my head, tossing it onto the floor.

A growl of approval came from him.

Malachi was on me in an instant, covering the now exposed skin with his warm body.

He pressed against me in his large, silk bed. I could tell from his touches, his kisses that he wanted this just as badly as I did.

"I love you, Malachi," I whispered against his mouth.

Between our panting breaths and desperate touches, it

wasn't long until there was nothing between us. Just our bodies together, blending in a way that lit up the darkest parts of my soul.

Malachi was mine.

I was his.

And that night, I surrendered to him fully.

CHAPTER 22
Malachi

"Malachi," Serefin's voice rang from outside the bedroom door, followed by a rapid knock. My eyelids shot open. "Malachi, are you in there?"

Jade stirred next to me, yanking the sheets up to her chin. My wings instinctively flared out, covering us both.

After last night, I never wanted her to leave this bed. I would never get enough of her laying next to me.

"Don't worry," I whispered. "It's just Ser." I then turned my attention to the door. It wasn't unlike him to be knocking this early. "Go away, Serefin!"

"Someone is here to see you," he persisted.

"Tell them to leave me alone," I said. I moved my hand to trace a long, delicate line down the side of Jade's perfect face. Her mouth twitched in a smile.

Serefin mumbled something I couldn't quite hear outside my door, then said, "It's the Paragon, Mal. Messengers from the Paragon are here and they're requesting to meet with you."

Jade's eyes shot back open. Any relaxation from her in that moment ripped away, like it was never there in the first place.

I couldn't deny that my heart rate sped up, too.

"Fine," I said after finding the words. "Keep them occupied. I'll be down in a moment."

I listened to his rushed footsteps as he walked away from the door, leaving Jade and I in the bedroom.

"What are they doing here?" Jade asked, sitting up in bed with a tight grip on the sheets. "What do they want? Why would they come all the way here?"

"Calm down," I said. "I'm sure it's nothing serious."

"Nothing serious?" she questioned. "How is the Paragon, our biggest enemy, by the way, showing up in our kingdom *not* serious?"

"If they wanted to cause us harm, half the kingdom would be dead by now. Trust me, Jade."

I rolled out of bed and began dressing myself, very aware of Jade's eyes watching my every move.

"Well?" I asked after a few seconds. "Are you coming?"

Her face flushed red, and she didn't say a word. She stayed put, holding the bed sheet tight to her chest. "I hate to break this to you, princess," I started, "but after last night, it's nothing I haven't seen before."

Jade rolled her eyes and threw one of the pillows at me, missing by a good foot.

"Turn around," she said.

After fully dressing myself, I listened, turning around while Jade got out of my bed and got herself dressed.

I didn't stop my mind from wandering to the soft curves

of her small body, and the way she felt in my arms last night. My chest warmed at the thought.

"Okay," she said, interrupting my thoughts after a few, agonizing minutes. "You can turn around now."

"Jade," I said as I turned around. "I know I said you have nothing to worry about, but I need you to listen to me."

"What's going on, Mal?"

I took a step toward her. How could I tell her, though? How could I get her to explain that I wasn't as calm as I appeared? The Paragon had haunted me for decades. If they were here, something was wrong.

Something was very wrong.

Panic threatened my senses.

What did they want? It was possible this had something to do with my new reign of Rewyth. Best case scenario, they wanted to express their condolences for my father. It was possible that they only meant to congratulate me on becoming king.

It was also possible they had heard that my human wife was actually not so ordinary, after all. Perhaps they had heard of her abilities. Did Seth turn her in? Did he go running to them about exactly what happened in Trithen?

Maybe they wanted to see her for themselves.

And that thought was the one that terrified me. The Paragon would not take Jade. They would not lay a single finger on her.

Because I knew, deep in my bones, that I would kill anyone who tried to take Jade away from me. Paragon or not.

"Tell me," she pushed. She closed the small distance between us and grabbed both of my wrists. "Tell me, Mal. What are you afraid of? What are we walking into?"

"Nothing," I lied. "It's going to be okay. I just need you to stay silent, and stay behind me. Okay? Don't trust them, whoever they are and whatever they want."

She nodded, as if she understood perfectly.

"I love you, Jade," I said, pressing a kiss on her forehead. "I'm not letting anyone hurt you."

"I know," she whispered back. "I know you won't."

I slid my hand into hers, and together, we began walking downstairs to meet our fate.

The castle looked different this early in the morning. It wasn't the same hustle of people that frequently filled these halls. No, the halls were practically empty, aside from a few servants who scurried in the shadows of the morning sun.

It was quiet. Saints, one might even say the castle was peaceful this early in the morning. That alone was an eerie thought, though, because I knew exactly how cruel this place really was. I didn't think any amount of quietness could make it truly peaceful.

Especially when I knew what awaited us.

Jade's hand was an anchor in mine, bringing me back to the moment. She had no idea what was awaiting her. Neither did I, though. Not really. It was possible that the Paragon had changed in the decades that I hadn't heard from them. Maybe they had changed their ways now. Maybe they ditched their methods of violence and blood for more peaceful methods.

I almost laughed at the thought. No, they most certainly hadn't changed for the better.

I pushed open the front doors to the castle, and my black wings immediately flared outward on instinct.

I tugged Jade's hand slightly, pulling her closer to my side.

Three black-hooded figures stood ahead of me, accompanied by Serefin, who was trying his best to distract them. Dozens of guards covered the surrounding area.

As if that would stop them.

"Ah," one of the figures acknowledged, stepping forward and pulling the hood from his head. "Here is our king."

He lowered his head just an inch. I knew that was the closest thing to a bow I was going to receive. I nodded in acknowledgement, and the figure returned to standing.

"I am told that you wish to speak with me," I stated. I didn't move from my position near the door.

The three guests looked at each other before the leader answered, "We have something we wish to discuss with you, yes. Is there somewhere more...private we can speak?"

I rolled my eyes. "If you have something to say to me, you can say it here. Everyone here can be trusted."

"Everyone?" he said. His dark eyes moved from me to Jade, who was now holding my arm.

My blood ran hot in my veins. "Yes," I barked.

"Fine," he said. "I suppose there is no harm in speaking of this here, then."

"Go on," I pushed.

"We heard word that you may have broken a treaty with the humans."

I waited for him to say more, but when nothing came, my jaw nearly dropped. That's what they came all this way for? "We broke no treaty."

"Well, we've heard otherwise. We've also heard whispers of something else happening over here in Rewyth."

There it was. The truth behind it all. "Really?" I asked,

keeping my voice as flat as possible. "And what could that possibly be?"

Say it. I thought. *Say it right now, and let's get it over with.*

The other two visitors slowly removed the hoods from their own heads.

My power rumbled within my veins. I was ready for a fight.

Jade tensed at my side. I knew she was ready, too.

"Why don't you tell us?" the leader asked. "Something on your conscience, King?"

I watched as Serefin's hand moved to his sword.

Him and each of the other guards.

"Have you heard of the peacemaker?" the leader asked when I said nothing. I knew he saw the threat against him. Part of me wanted to test him, to see if he had any power that matched my own.

Or that matched Jade's.

Would the Paragon send ungifted messengers? Knowing that they were going to pose a threat to us?

Maybe they wanted to push us. Maybe they wanted to keep pushing and pushing until they saw what Jade was really made of.

"Peacemaker?" I repeated. "Hmm, I can't really say that I have."

"Interesting," the leader stepped forward, only half a step. "Because we have resources telling us that the peacemaker is alive, and that she looks terribly similar to your human wife."

My jaw tightened. "That's quite a statement."

"It is, indeed."

"Is that the reason you came all the way here?" I asked,

"To inquire on the similarities between my wife and this said peacemaker?"

The leader smiled. "Not quite. You see, the Paragon, as you may know, is in charge of many things. One of these things is maintaining the power balance amongst fae, witches, and humans."

I could feel Jade's anger rising beside me.

The man continued, "If the rumors we have been hearing are true, your wife could greatly upset this balance."

"Weird," I chirped. "I wasn't aware that the mighty Paragon was in the business of listening to petty gossip."

"When that gossip involves the possible downfall of our system, we listen."

Their words lingered in the air, landing the final blow to the real reason they showed up.

I let go of Jade's hand and took one step forward. Everyone's eyes glued onto me. "Do we have a problem here, gentleman?"

The three of them stood there, staring at me. They knew the answer. I knew what they were going to say.

"We've had a problem since the day your wife was born, King Malachi."

Jade exhaled loudly behind me. "I would think very carefully about what you say next. This is my kingdom, and you're threatening my queen."

"We didn't come here to threaten anyone. We came here to see if the rumors were true."

My power ran hot in my body, ready to take these men down with a single thought. "How exactly do you plan on doing that?"

A single threatening word from them, and my power

would wipe them out. Their bodies would never find their way back to the Paragon.

"We were hoping you would do us the small favor of exhibiting your wife's powers upon our request."

I laughed. I *actually laughed*. Were they serious?

"And why would I do that? So you could rip her away from here and take her back to your leader? Or is it for your own sick interests?"

"It's in your best interest."

"Really? How is that possibly in my best interest?"

"Mal," Jade warned from behind me. I ignored her. How dare these three march in here and demand to see Jade's power? Did they really think I would roll over and let them do whatever they wanted?

This was my kingdom. It was *my* job to keep the people of Rewyth safe.

Including Jade.

I found myself wishing Esther were here.

But I quickly shook it off.

"Look," the leader said as he lowered his voice. "I understand that you're trying to protect her. But we have very strict orders to discover if your human wife really possesses power or not. We can't leave here without seeing her gifts."

"And if we refuse to cooperate?"

"Then we won't be the ones coming down here next time. You'll be hearing from Silas."

The blood rushed from my face. *Silas.*

"What did you just say?" I asked. My fists clenched at my sides.

"If we don't deliver news about your wife, Silas will come here himself. And he won't be so peaceful."

"You call showing up here and threatening my wife *peaceful?*"

"We wish no harm on your wife, King Malachi. We only wish to discover the truth."

"The truth? You're looking for the truth of an ancient prophecy that could be complete bullshit, and you're hoping to find the truth from my wife?"

"Don't make this harder than it needs to be."

I looked at Serefin, who only clenched his jaw in response. *Get ready.* "This is *my* kingdom," I declared. "I will not say that again. I plan on making this very difficult for you. If you want something from me or my wife, you'll have to take it yourselves. I'm not giving you anything."

The three men looked at their surroundings, likely sizing us up to see how easily they could take us.

Not happening.

The man in front opened his black cloak and reached inside. I half expected a rush of magic to take us out. They were from the mighty Paragon, after all. But instead, he only pulled out a small dagger.

Every guard in the vicinity pulled weapons of their own. I backed up, reclaiming my spot next to Jade.

Although I was certain that not a single one of my guards would let these fools touch her.

"Really?" I asked. "You come here with nothing but a handheld weapon?"

"Like I said. I don't intend on making this harder than it needs to be."

The three of them spread out, just slightly. Enough to let me know that they were actually considering making a move.

"Jade, go inside," I demanded.

"Sending her inside isn't going to stop us."

"Is that another threat?"

"It's a warning, King Malachi. Silas gave us these orders. You know what that means."

I listened as Jade's footsteps grew quieter and quieter as she retreated into the castle behind me. I thanked the Saints that she listened this time. Being in the castle wouldn't make her safe, but she didn't need to be near this.

"Leave now," I warned. "That's a warning. And it's the only one you'll get."

"You know we can't do that."

"You know I'll kill you if you don't."

"I know you're a powerful man," he spoke, spinning his weapon in his hand. "I know you have a special gift, King Malachi. But you know that Silas won't allow us to return with nothing. So this battle is a chance I'm willing to put my wages on."

My heart began pounding in my chest. Not in a nervous way. I knew this would barely be a fight. These three would just be three more bodies on my list of casualties.

For Jade, I would gladly add them.

For Jade, I would do whatever it took.

Serefin and Doromir stepped around the back of the group. The three visitors were now surrounded.

There was no going back.

The leader turned to the other two and whispered, "Go find the girl."

And those four words were enough to start a war.

"Kill them all," I ordered.

My power flared in their direction. I allowed the tendrils of magic to drop all three of them to the ground. The ones that moved to follow Jade were now clutching and clawing at their insides, screeching in indescribable pain.

They deserved worse. They deserved much worse than pain.

"Serefin," I ordered, "end it."

Serefin's sword came down on the left one's neck, severing it with one motion.

One threat down.

The leader began groaning, clearly trying to speak. I pulled back my strong tendrils of power, just enough so I could hear his last words.

"They'll come for her," he said through gritted teeth, still in pieces on the ground. "They'll come for her and you know it. She'll never be safe."

"Why?" I demanded. "What will they do with her?"

He laughed, but pain laced every sound. "They'll do what they wanted to do with you. They'll use her power for themselves. The balance must be maintained."

Serefin's sword came down once more, and the leader flinched as his last shred of hope died along with his last companion.

"We'll kill anyone who tries to take her," I declared.

I didn't wait for Serefin to kill him. I pulled my own sword from my hip and brought it down, hard, on the last of our unwanted guests.

When I finally looked up, everyone was staring at me. Watching me. Waiting for our next move.

"Keep this to ourselves," I said to the guards. "Serefin, begin preparing our army. This is not the only time we'll be hearing from the Paragon."

"They'll come for her," Serefin replied. Something harsh

crossed his features. That was rare for Serefin. "We need to protect Jade. It's too dangerous for her here."

I considered his words. "Jade's been running for a long time, Ser. This is her home now. Spread the word. If anyone approaches this kingdom with intent to harm my wife, they will be struck down on sight."

CHAPTER 23

Jade

Malachi stormed inside and, without looking at me, grabbed me from where I had been listening just within the castle doors and began pulling me along with him.

"Malachi," I said, careful with my words. He had just killed them. The messenger from the Paragon, he killed them all. Adrenaline buzzed through my body. "They're coming for me, aren't they?"

"Nobody's coming for you, Jade."

We passed dozens of guards in the halls, everyone now moving with a certain seriousness that I hadn't noticed before.

Would they stand for me? Would they protect me? Lay down their own lives for me?

"Mal, maybe I should–"

"No," I interrupted. The grip on his arm tightened as he pulled me into an emptier hallway. "Don't even say what I know you're about to say."

"It's just that if we–"

"Stop!" he argued. Malachi spun me in his grip, moving to press my back lightly against the stone wall of the hallway. "I'm going to say this once, Jade, so you better be listening. You're not going anywhere. I'm not letting anyone use you for this stupid prophecy, okay? Esther can't have you, the Paragon can't have you. Saints, *nobody* can have you. Is that clear?"

My stomach flipped in excitement. Malachi protecting me was nothing new, but it still shocked me that he was willing to give up everything for me. A *human*.

His wife. His queen. The peacemaker.

I stopped myself from thinking anything more. At the end of the day, I was still a human.

Malachi's eyes scanned my face, searching for any type of reaction.

So I answered in a way that words couldn't. I moved my hands to his face, gripping tightly and turning his head so his eyes were level with mine. "If you are willing to risk your kingdom, your reign, and your people for me," I paused, staring into those deep forests of eyes, "I won't stop you. But I don't think I'm worth saving, Mal. It's too much trouble–"

Malachi shut me up with a kiss.

His mouth moved against mine, the warmth from him moving across my entire body. His hands slipped around my waist, holding me tightly to him as he continued to kiss me.

Was this how it was going to be from now on? Desperate kisses in the shadows of the castle?

When he pulled away, his eyes were serious. "You are my queen, Jade Weyland. I will protect you with my life."

My heart erupted in a love I could not even fathom.

"Then I suppose we should talk about how in the Saints

we plan on defeating the Paragon."

He grabbed my hand and gently began leading me down the hallway, in the direction of his bedroom.

Or was it our bedroom now?

"Before we do that," he started. "I think it's time I tell you a story."

"I'm not sure now is really the best time for st–"

"A story about my time with the Paragon."

In the peaceful hideaway of the bedroom, Malachi began from the beginning. He told me about when the Paragon came to him for the very first time, demanding that they were required to observe exactly how powerful each new gift was.

And Malachi's gift was particularly impressive.

Malachi was honored at first. Honored that such a powerful entity wanted to know him. Wanted to see what he could do.

He had no problem showing them what his power could do.

It was around that time, however, that his own father also began learning about just how powerful he really was. His father discovered that Malachi could become much more than a boy.

He was no longer just a son, no. With the expansion of his gift, and with years of training, Malachi became the most powerful weapon in all of Rewyth.

This attracted more and more attention to him, specifically from the Paragon. They tried building a genuine relationship at first. They explained that they would help Malachi, that they would take him away from his father who clearly didn't have his best interests in mind and they would harbor his talents like they do for other gifted individuals.

Malachi's eyes lit up as he explained all this. This was a side of him that I hadn't seen before. A side of him that I never even knew existed.

"I trusted them," he explained. "I was young and naive and I wanted a way out, so I trusted them."

Pain flashed across his features.

I reached across the short distance between us and grabbed his hand, holding tight. "And they betrayed you?" I asked.

"Not at first, no," he started. "At the beginning, they upheld every promise they had made. I packed my things and moved to the mountains, so deep that even my father could not find me if he sent an entire army after me. The mountains are a different place. They're secluded and hidden from all prying eyes."

The smile that flickered across his face was one of both joy and grief.

"But that didn't last," he explained. "Silas was the one who took me in. He nurtured me. I was so young, this was decades ago now."

My blood froze in my veins.

"Silas?" I repeated. "Why haven't you mentioned him before?"

Mal's eyes darkened. "He wasn't worth mentioning."

"And he's the leader?" I asked. "Of the Paragon?"

Malachi took a deep breath before answering, "Yes. He is. We were friends for a while, believe it or not. He guided me while I became powerful. He helped me realize who I could be in this world. But that was before I decided to leave. That was before I learned just how much they wanted from me."

I shook my head. "I have a hard time believing the

Paragon, being as power hungry as they are, enjoyed the fact that you wanted to leave."

"They tried to convince me to stay. They offered me a home there, and a position in the Paragon. But I was the heir to Rewyth. I had duties back in the castle. After years, it was time for me to return home."

He stayed quiet for a few moments.

"Do you think Silas will try to kill me?" I asked, finally speaking the questions we had both been thinking.

Malachi looked me in the eyes when he answered, "If killing you will give him more power, I have no doubt he'll take the chance."

Great.

"We'll prepare for a full-on attack from the Paragon," he said. "I'll reach out to our allies and see who will come to our aid. We won't let them take you, Jade."

"Rewyth really has allies?" I asked. "I guess after what happened in Trithen I didn't think that was possible."

Malachi smiled. "My father had many enemies, but it's time I start cleaning up his mess. If it's true that you are the secret to this prophecy of power, they'll come to our aid."

"Thank you," I said. "For doing this. For caring."

Malachi reached up and tucked a stray piece of hair behind my ear. "You didn't ask for any of this, Jade," he stated. "To be honest, I'm not even sure how you're still standing."

"It's not without difficulty," I replied. Tessa's words rang loudly in my mind.

Do you feel lucky to be alive?

CHAPTER 24
Malachi

Over the next three weeks, hundreds of fae came to our aid. I was surprised at first, I'll admit, that anyone was willing to come help us. It took days for our messengers to get back to me, and by then I was almost certain that everyone would decline our call for help.

But one by one, armies began showing up.

We filled every possible room in the castle, and the overflow of men camped out in the nearby fields.

We were a force to be reckoned with.

I stood on the tallest balcony of our castle, taking in the view of hundreds of allies when the door opened behind me.

I spun around, half-hoping it would be Jade.

Eli.

Eli had certainly kept his distance from me since Fynn's death. I didn't mind it. It only meant that I could keep pushing away these tough conversations.

"Brother," I greeted.

He came to stand next to me, looking out onto our kingdom. "You've had quite the turnout," he stated.

"I can't say I'm not surprised."

"New king. New rule. New hope," he said. Something in the way he said *hope* made me tense.

Did Eli still have hope? After Fynn's death, did he believe in a better world for us?

"How have you been, brother?" I asked.

Eli only shook his head. "I'm surviving. Trying to find the reason for all of this."

My heart twisted. "It will get better, Eli," I said. "I promise you it gets easier."

"How long did it take for you?" he asked. The words shocked me, but I knew he was coming from a place of genuine curiosity. "How long did it take for you to be okay after your previous wives died?"

I tried not to look shocked. It wasn't every day that my past wives were mentioned. Before Jade, I wasn't sure a single day would go by that I didn't think of them.

Now, though, they were only distant memories.

It's both relieving and heart-wrenching, that time can wipe away memories and emotions piece by piece.

Day by day.

"A while," I answered. "It took a long time."

I didn't dare compare my previous companions with the relationship that Eli had with his twin brother Fynn.

My wives had each been different in indescribable ways. Each of them human, each of them fragile, yet they all held a different place in my heart.

Especially when each of them were slaughtered while I stood by and watched.

I hadn't cared about any of them like I had cared about Jade.

Eli and Fynn had been inseparable since birth.

I could still hear Eli's scream that day when he found Fynn dead on the battlefield.

"We'll make them pay," I said, not able to find any other words. "We'll make them all pay for what they have taken from us."

Eli placed his hand on my shoulder. It was the closest thing to comfort that any of my brothers had ever shown me. "I believe in you, Malachi. I know you'll protect us. I know you'll make them suffer for what they have done."

"Thank you, Eli."

He turned to leave, but stopped before opening the door. "Someone is here to see you. They're waiting in your private dining room."

And then he was gone.

I waited for a few moments, taking in the view of the sun setting in the distance, casting a red glow on everything beneath me.

This was my kingdom. My responsibility.

Eli was right. Together, we would make them pay.

We would make them all pay.

When I arrived in the dining room, I was greeted with a large hug. "Carlyle," I breathed a sigh of relief that I was being greeted by a friend, not an enemy. "It's nice to see you."

Carlyle pulled away and clapped me on the shoulder. "It's been too long, friend. I only wish we were coming together in better circumstances."

I motioned to the table, and we both took a seat.

"When I heard you were being threatened by the Paragon..."

He didn't have to finish the sentence. He knew just how brutal the wrath of the Paragon could be.

"Thank you for coming," I said. "After everything my father did, I wasn't expecting much."

Carlyle nodded, words unsaid passed between us.

When I first met Carlyle, I was on strict orders from my father. My father wanted what he always wanted—power. It didn't take me more than a few minutes with Carlyle, though, to understand that he wasn't the monster my father had tried to convince me he was.

Carlyle was a kind man and a gracious leader. I didn't kill him that day, like my father ordered.

Instead, Carlyle and I became allies.

And it appeared as though he was returning the favor.

"I've brought my best men, but I hope for your wife's sake you have a plan on how you're going to take on the Paragon. They're the Paragon for a reason, and it's not because they are weak or easily defeated."

"Trust me, I know. But at the end of the day, everyone has a weakness. I just need to find theirs."

"The Paragon doesn't show weakness easily. You know this more than anyone."

"I'm desperate, Carlyle. If I can't find a way to stop them when they come, they'll take her."

Carlyle's eyes darkened. I didn't expect him to fully understand the situation I was in, but he was a caring person. Perhaps he would have an idea.

"You have an impressive amount of manpower here, Malachi, but is that enough? What happens when they come at you with power? It's been years since you've last seen them. They could be much stronger now..."

"Or weaker."

"I suppose that is a possibility."

We both took a long breath. I leaned back in my chair, running my hands across my face. *Think, Malachi.* There had to be an easier way out of this mess.

Carlyle set both of his hands on the table. "I don't mean to be presumptuous, Malachi, but I've heard whispers of your mother. And I've heard she's here in this kingdom."

"She's lucky she's still alive after what she did to me."

"Maybe. But instead of rotting away somewhere under our feet, you could use her."

I shook my head. I would be lying if the thought hadn't crossed my mind. But Esther couldn't be trusted. I felt no remorse about locking her in the dungeons. She deserved much worse. "It's too risky," I admitted. "She turned on me once, what's to say she won't do it again?"

"If the witch faces death," Carlyle said, dropping his voice to a low whisper, "she will have no choice but to comply."

"It's not that simple."

"Isn't it?" Carlyle pushed. "Right now, it's looking like you need all of the help you can get. You're a new king, that makes you weak enough. You have your power, and you have men that are willing to fight for you. But the Paragon will come with every ounce of magic they've got. It's in your best interest to do the same."

"She tried to kill me, Carlyle. Her own son."

"We've all done insane things to survive."

I let his words sink in, and I tried to fight the wave of anger that came from listening to them. Yes, we have all done insane things to survive. I couldn't even begin to count the number of times I had done something desperate to get out of dying. Holding a blade to my wife's throat being one of them.

But Esther wanted Jade's power. Esther was loyal to her bloodline of witches, even with them dead. She did not want us fae to fulfill this prophecy and become the most powerful with our magic.

She did not want magic returned to the fae.

But the only other option was the Paragon using the power. And they already had enough.

"I suppose it's worth a shot," I finally admitted through gritted teeth. "But she's been in the dungeon for weeks now. I can't imagine she's much stronger than a human at this point."

"A weak witch with some power is better than nothing."

Saints, he was right.

"You don't happen to know of any powerful witch bloodlines that would be willing to come to our aid, do you?" I asked, only half-joking.

Carlyle smiled, the wrinkles around his eyes multiplying. "If I did, we wouldn't hear the word Paragon ever again."

CHAPTER 25
Jade

"Just sit down and shut up, okay?" I hissed to my father, motioning for him to sit at the large wooden table that stretched the length of the busy dining hall.

He nodded and stepped over the bench, Tessa sliding in next to him. It had been too long since the three of us had eaten together, and with everything going on, I wasn't sure I was going to get another chance.

Besides, after the last time my father and I encountered each other in this dining hall, I felt the need to redeem myself.

We could behave, couldn't we? For one meal, we could behave like a normal family for *one* meal.

Normal family. I almost laughed at the thought. I sat at the bench opposite of Tessa and my father, and began eating my meal in silence. My sister did the same. It was our father who sat there, hardly moving and staring at everyone around us.

"Are you going to eat?" I asked him after a few minutes of silence. "Your food will get cold."

"I find it hard to eat when we are surrounded by enemies," he mumbled, hardly audible.

"Father," Tessa warned in a low voice. I held my hand up to stop her.

After coming moments away from erupting into ash the last time my father and I fought, I was trying my best to keep my temper under control. He didn't need to fear me, and he certainly didn't need to fear the others.

"These aren't our enemies, father," I explained calmly, looking into his blood-shot eyes. "They're here to fight for me."

He shrugged uncomfortably. It was hard not to see my father as the weak and confused man he really was. Hidden beneath the decades of losing himself in ale, was a simple man who wanted to survive.

A man who had lived a terrible, difficult life.

A man who had lost his wife.

Who had nothing to live for anymore.

When he wasn't running around creating a list of enemies for himself, he was simply trying to live for the next day.

"For you?" he questioned. "They're fighting for you?"

"Yes, father," I said, taking another bite of my stew. "They tell me I am special, remember? I have a special power and people are trying to take it. So they are helping me. They're protecting me."

This was the sixth time I had to explain that to him. The second and the third time, I was annoyed. But not anymore.

He still looked confused at my words, but didn't push the conversation any more. "So," I started, desperate for any sort of conversation, "have you two been missing home?"

"Are you kidding?" Tessa replied with a sudden burst of

energy. "You'll have to drag my dead body back there. I should have been living here all along!"

My father snorted in response.

"Wow," I started. "That's pretty much the exact opposite of the response I was expecting from you."

Tessa shoved her mouth with another bite of food, barely swallowing before adding, "I can't remember the last time I was hungry. Seriously, I think I've eaten more here in Rewyth than I have my entire life."

I smiled at my sister, but my stomach flipped. It was a joke, but it held a wicked truth.

Tessa was being taken care of here for maybe the first time in her entire life. "Yeah," I responded. "I know how you feel."

My father dropped his fork and shoved his tray away from him with a grunt.

I was all for keeping my temper cool, but he had no right to get angry over that.

He wasn't there for us. No matter what the reasons were, and no matter how messed up a man he had become, he didn't take care of us.

I did. *I* fed our family. *I* watched over Tessa. *I* put clothes on our backs. He wasn't allowed to get angry over that truth.

"Something to add, father?" I asked. I knew I was pushing him, but that dark shadow deep inside of me couldn't stop myself. "Because if you have something to say, you should just say it."

Tessa's eyes dropped to her food. She had always been the non-confrontational one of us.

"You two act like I am nothing in this family," my father whispered.

Normally, I would have snapped right back. But Tessa looked at me with a surprise in her eyes that set me back.

Because we both knew that was the most *real* sentence my father had said in years.

"We did a lot without you, I didn't think that was a secret," I said, barely a whisper.

"And you think I was off having a great time? I suffered just as much as you two, if not more so. I suffered every single day!"

Tessa and I didn't say a word.

My father placed both of his boney, frail hands on the table. They trembled.

"I am not a blind man. I know you two have not had a great life. But neither have I. I have–"

He paused to take a deep, long breath. I could have sworn he began blinking back tears.

Tessa's foot tapped against mine under the table.

"We love you, father," Tessa caved after a few seconds. She placed a hand on his shoulder and leaned in slightly. My father didn't back away from it. "We don't say it enough, but it's true."

My father smiled, but his eyes didn't meet mine.

I unclenched my jaw, realizing it had been clenched the entire time he was talking.

I wasn't going to repeat Tessa. I didn't need to. I can't remember my father ever saying he loved me. I can't remember ever saying it to him, either.

I wasn't about to start now.

"Well," he said, clearing his throat. "I'm exhausted. I should get to bed."

Without looking at either of us, our father stood from the table and walked away.

Neither of us followed after him.

"That was weird," I mumbled to Tessa.

"He's been...different lately," she explained. "He hasn't been drinking. He's been talking more. Screaming less."

"That doesn't sound like him."

"No," she said. "It doesn't. Maybe he's realizing that this place is better for him than he originally thought."

Tessa looked at me with more hope than I had in my entire body. "Yeah," I agreed, knowing it was not likely that my father would ever change. "It's possible."

We returned to our meals, although after the conversation we just had, I wasn't hungry in the slightest.

"Who died?" Adeline's voice caused me to drop my fork. She slapped her tray down on the wooden table and slid into the bench beside me, sitting so close that her arm brushed up beside mine.

"What?" I asked.

"You two look like you're mourning a death. What's with the sad faces?"

"Nothing," Tessa and I said in unison.

"Well, fix those sad faces," she insisted. "Because we're going to have some fun."

"What are you talking about?" I asked.

"We're doing something for ourselves," she stated. "We're heading into town. Let's go now before I change my mind."

Tessa's face lit up in a mixture of excitement and fear that matched my own. "Town?" she questioned.

Adeline nodded with a mischievous twinkle in her eye. "Follow me."

I didn't hesitate for a second. Tessa and I practically jumped from the table and followed Adeline out of the castle.

She led us past the hidden lagoon in the woods and through a long and skinny dirt path, sometimes walking so quickly we had to jog to catch up. "Are you sure this is safe?" I questioned as we ventured further. "I mean, is it common to head into town whenever you want?"

Adeline flipped her long hair over her shoulder. "It's plenty safe," she answered, "but I wouldn't necessarily go telling Malachi about this little adventure. You know how he gets."

Tessa's eyes darted between Adeline and me, but she didn't say anything.

"And you go into town frequently? What if someone recognizes us?" Adeline didn't answer. Instead, she kept walking forward, further and further down the path. A few moments later, Adeline ducked off the path and into the tree line. "Adeline!" I hissed. "Adeline, where are you going?" I grabbed Tessa's arm and stayed with her on the path.

"Relax," she said as she stepped back into view a few seconds later. "We need these."

She passed us each a hooded cloak. "Seriously?" I asked. "You just hide these in the trees?"

"Where else am I going to hide them?" she questioned.

I helped Tessa adjust her cloak before covering my own head. After what happened with Kara in the hallway, I was fairly certain I could defend myself against a fae, but an entire town full of them? That would be a death wish.

We had to be cautious. With a target on my back, nowhere would be safe.

Adeline led us onward, through the trees and on the same narrow path, until the trees grew thinner and thinner.

Squinting ahead, I could make out the rough shape of small stone buildings. "Is that it?" I asked.

"It sure is!"

"It's smaller than I imagined."

Adeline laughed. "Trust me, it's much bigger once you're down there."

We continued walking with Tessa trailing silently behind us. I could feel the excitement buzzing off of her.

The stone buildings became bigger and bigger, and in just a few minutes, the streets of Rewyth became clear.

They were no longer smaller than I had imagined. The buildings themselves may not have been castle-like, but each fae we passed practically dripped in jewels and riches.

The town was magnificent.

I didn't let go of Tessa's hand, even as she gawked at each fancy new item we passed.

"Here we are," Adeline said, stepping into a doorway of one of the shops.

"Where are we?" I asked. "What is this place?"

The three of us walked inside, and the door closed behind us with the ring of a small bell.

A woman stepped forward with her gaze locked on Adeline. Her eyes held a certain warmth that instantly made me feel comfortable.

"This is Vespera. She's my favorite dressmaker in the kingdom. We're dressing up today ladies, my treat. The coronation ball is tomorrow and we'll be looking our very best!"

Tessa squealed in excitement as the realization hit her. I

reminded myself to stay calm. "We're going to a ball? And you're buying us dresses?"

"No, silly," Vespera answered for her. She was a thin, pale fae with slender wings. She had numerous piercings accenting her face, and her hand was thin as she stuck it out to me to shake. "We're making them from scratch."

Breath escaped me. I could have never dreamed of having my own dress back home, much less having one made for me.

Living in Rewyth, I had been given many dresses to wear. But none of them felt like mine. None of them felt like they were for me.

I knew Tessa felt the same way. Dresses meant much more to her than they meant to me. They always had. For her, this would be a dream.

This would be everything.

Adeline must have known that, too. This would be a life-long memory for Tessa, even if she had to return back to the human lands once this was all over.

"Thank you, Adeline," I said, motioning to Tessa as she began running her hands over the different fabrics that lined the wall. "This is too kind."

Adeline only nodded. "What are friends for? Besides, I think your sister could use some distraction."

My heart tightened watching Tessa's entire spirit shine. She had never asked for much. I knew she always wanted more when we lived back home, but she knew. She knew I was doing everything I could. She also knew that new dresses, warm shoes, or a nice coat were out of the picture for us.

But this? I could give her this. I could let Adeline do this for her.

For us.

We spent hours in that shop. Tessa tried every single fabric combination, and Vespera eagerly debated which colors looked best with her light skin and caramel hair.

Adeline and I sat back and watched, laughing at each time Vespera stuck her with a sewing pin.

It wasn't too long until Tessa stood in front of us with a full, brand-new dress.

"You look beautiful, Tessa," I said as I gawked at her.

Tears welled in her eyes as she stared at her own reflection. She looked stunning. It was a shame what life could do to such raw magnificence.

She looked like royalty.

In another life, she would have been. I knew it.

"I can't believe I get to keep this," Tessa whispered. "I can't believe this is mine."

"You deserve it," Adeline spoke up. "That dress belongs on someone as beautiful as you. And now you'll have something to wear to the coronation ball!"

Tessa glowed.

We spent the next few hours running through the town, ignoring each of our problems. It felt nice, pretending to be three normal girls in Rewyth.

Tessa loved every minute of it.

But like all good things in my life, it had to end.

Later that night, after the three of us snuck back unnoticed, I crawled into my warm, comfortable bed. The memory of seeing Tessa smile at herself in that dress replayed in my mind until I drifted off to sleep.

Cold, scrawny hands gripped my wrists. My eyes shot open in the darkness, and I found Esther kneeling before me.

"Esther?" I questioned. "What are you doing here?"

Her long white hair looked cleaner than the last time I saw her. She appeared healthier, too. "We need to talk."

I realized I was no longer lying in my bed. I wasn't in my bedroom at all, actually. I was in the dungeons, where Esther should have been chained up.

But she wasn't.

"Talk about what?" I asked, pushing myself up from the cold stone ground. How did I get down here?

"The Paragon is coming for you, child." Her voice grew tight with desperation.

"I know that. It's not exactly a secret."

"I told you I could help you get out of this. I can."

"Okay? Are you finally willing to share what you know?" She hesitated. "Why are you so afraid of telling me?" I pushed. She had been keeping information from Malachi and I ever since we left Trithen. It was time for her to start talking.

"I'm not afraid of you," she defended, "but Malachi won't like what I'm going to say."

I was officially interested. What was Esther so afraid of telling Malachi? What did she know?

"Whatever it is, he'll be happy if it saves my life. Just tell me, Esther."

"Fine," she sighed. She leaned in. "It's about a man named Silas. Has Malachi mentioned him?"

I fought through my brain fog to recall any mention of the name. Silas was the same man Malachi mentioned that practi-

cally raised him in the Paragon. Did Esther know? Did she know Malachi's history with Silas? I decided to play dumb. "No," I answered. "I haven't heard of him."

"Silas is the leader of the Paragon. He makes the rules. He calls the shots. If someone wants your power, it's him. If members from the Paragon are showing up at our kingdom, it's under his orders."

"And why are you telling me this?" I pushed. "Why should I care about a man I've never heard of?"

"Because," she started. "Silas and I grew up together."

I blinked. "What? You grew up with the Paragon?"

Malachi and Esther had ties to the Paragon? This was becoming too odd.

She shook her head. "It wasn't the Paragon back then. Silas was just a man. He wanted peace, and that's where it all began. That's where everything began, Jade."

"So you're friends with the leader of the Paragon? This could change everything, Esther. Why haven't you brought this up before? Why hide it?"

She leaned back slightly, looking away from me in the darkness. "I wouldn't exactly call us friends."

The ground beneath us shook.

"What is this, Esther? You're in my dream?"

"I can't stay long. Don't tell Malachi we spoke. When the Paragon comes for you, I'll talk with Silas. I'll make him understand."

I didn't have time to ask her any more questions. My vision faded to black, and everything went dark.

CHAPTER 26
Jade

The coronation ball was more of a formality than anything. The castle wanted to celebrate Malachi becoming King of Rewyth, and any excuse for the fae of the castle to drink and party was seldom passed up.

I glanced at Tessa. Her bright blue gown practically illuminated against her skin. She had never been to a ball before, much less a fae coronation. Nerves tickled my stomach, but Tessa appeared to be calm. Calmer than usual, actually. She held her chin high and walked with promise as we approached the doors to the ballroom.

"Stay with me as long as you can," I whispered. "When the coronation ends, I'll come find you. Stay out of trouble, and find Serefin or Adeline if you need anything."

Tessa found my hand and gave it a quick squeeze. "I'll be okay," she replied. "You don't need to worry about me."

I would never stop worrying about Tessa, but she didn't need to hear that. Not before the party. Especially with Esther visiting my dreams, I had my guard up. There could never be a simple, boring event around Rewyth.

We approached the coronation, and the castle began stirring with life. Music flowed from the room, echoing off the stone walls and shaking my bones. The room already moved with fae dancing and celebrating, eager to participate in the event.

"Long live the King!" a few shouted as one song came to an end. The long strings of music easily flowed into another, and the dancers easily picked up where they left off.

I spotted Adeline and Malachi in the distance, both talking to fae I had never seen before. I couldn't help but notice how formal they both appeared—much different than the versions of them I had grown to know. "Over there," I whispered to Tessa.

She took the hint, and together we worked our way through the crowd.

Malachi's eyes lit up as soon as he saw us. "Jade," he nodded. He and Adeline dismissed their guests and turned to give us their full attention. "Tessa, you are both looking lovely this evening."

Tessa's face turned bright pink, but she mumbled a thanks and dropped her head in greeting.

"You're looking well yourself," I said to Mal. "And you're stunning as ever," I nodded to Adeline. "Serefin is a lucky man."

Adeline stepped forward and smacked my arm lightly. "I have no idea what you're talking about."

Malachi and Tessa both laughed. "What?" I asked, holding my hands out in surrender. "We all see the way you two look at each other! You're not as sneaky as you think you are."

Adeline rolled her eyes and grabbed ahold of Tessa's hand.

"Tessa and I are going to enjoy the party. Find us after the coronation," she whispered. "And good luck."

I couldn't understand why we would need luck to get through the ceremony, but I watched as Mal nodded—signaling it was okay for them to leave us.

The hair on the back of my neck stood up. "Adeline will protect her," Mal whispered. His warm hand found my lower back. "There's no need to worry."

I watched them walk away until they were swallowed by the crowd of dancing silver wings.

"I don't like leaving her," I admitted. "She's too fragile. Any fae who messes with her could ruin her."

Malachi clicked his tongue. "Humans," he whispered close to my ear. "Fickle little things."

I elbowed him in the stomach lightly, but he only laughed harder. "Let's get this coronation over with," I whispered. "I'm growing tired of these ridiculous dresses."

When I turned to face Mal, his eyes were dark with hidden emotion. I watched as they flickered down to my dress —to the tight corset that exposed a good portion of my chest. "I don't think I'll ever grow tired of these *ridiculous* dresses." His hand tickled my shoulder as he traced the thin, sheer fabric there. "Care for a dance?"

I was shaking my head before I could even open my mouth. "No way," I declined. "Not in front of all these people."

"These are your people now," he pointed out. "And you didn't seem to have a problem dancing together at our wedding. Or at the festival in Trithen..." His voice grew thick as he took a tiny step closer.

I looked away from Mal and glanced around the room.

Fae scattered throughout the room, but nobody seemed to be paying us special attention.

"One dance," I agreed after a few seconds. "But that's it."

A satisfied smile spread across his face. Malachi took my hand without a word and pulled me, walking backward, to the source of the music.

The melody was not slow by any means, but Malachi didn't seem to care. He held my hand and pulled my body gently to his, caressing my lower back as he began swaying.

"The King of Shadows dances much more than I would have expected," I teased.

Malachi's smile only grew as he spun me in a circle. "This is my official coronation," he replied. "I've been waiting to be officially recognized as the King for decades now. This should be one of the happiest days of my existence."

"It is well deserved," I replied. "The kingdom is in great hands."

His eyes searched mine as if they were looking for a lie in my words. But they found none.

I meant those words. Malachi was going to change the fate of the kingdom with his rule, I could feel that much deep in my bones. He was powerful, yet he held so much light inside of him. He had buried it in a place that was hard to find, but it was there. And I saw the light in him every time his eyes met mine.

The music continued to play, but I no longer listened to it. The fae around us seemed to disappear as I admired him. Malachi must have felt this, too. His hands tightened on my body. The small amount of space between us vanished.

And we danced.

It was more than one dance, but I didn't care. I let him

guide me through the ballroom with ease, enjoying every second of our time together.

Minutes ticked by. I didn't think about Tessa, Esther, my magic, or anything else. I just let my husband hold me in the crowded room of our people.

It wasn't until the music stopped entirely that I noticed the fae around us.

Malachi stiffened as he, too, noticed it. The crowd around us stood in a semi-circle, watching us.

Blood rushed to my face. "Why is everyone staring at us?" I whispered to Mal. His hand never left mine. If he was in any way embarrassed, he didn't show it.

"Because I am the King of Rewyth," he said, only loud enough so I could hear. "They're waiting for us."

He cleared his throat and, without letting go of me, began walking to the throne. I followed. The silent crowd parted ways as we moved through it, and when we reached the bottom of the steps that led to the throne, Malachi paused.

Serefin and another guard stood next to the throne.

Another man, one I recognized from the court dinner, stepped forward onto the stage. "Fae of Rewyth," he announced. "Today we gather to commence the coronation of our new king, Malachi Weyland." Malachi bowed his head slightly as we waited for him to continue. "Malachi, please join me."

Malachi squeezed my hand once before letting go. I tried to ignore the wave of loneliness I felt as he stepped forward to stand before his throne and his kingdom.

He stood with his shoulders back and his chin high, like he deserved to be there all along.

"King Malachi," the guard announced. "Today we gather

here to officially name you, Malachi Weyland, as the leader and king of this great fae kingdom, the Kingdom of Rewyth."

Cheers erupted in the crowd around us. Malachi stared straight ahead.

The guard held a large crown covered in bright red rubies before Malachi before continuing. "By accepting this crown, you promise to uphold the values of this kingdom. You promise to protect this kingdom by any means necessary, and you promise to lead the citizens of this kingdom to live peaceful and safe lives. You hereby recognize the sacrifices of our ancestors, and the lives they gave up to protect our people. You swear to maintain the utmost priority of defending this kingdom against any and all enemies. Do you accept this oath?"

Malachi's jaw tightened. "I accept this oath."

The guard lowered the crown onto Mal's head. Serefin stepped forward and secured the velvet red robe around him.

And when Malachi lifted his head again, he was officially the King of Rewyth.

"Long live the King!" Serefin cheered.

"Long live the King!" the crowd repeated. The cheers began once more, filling the room with their support.

Pride welled in my chest. Malachi had been a king since his father was killed, and maybe even before that. But this was the first time his kingdom officially saw him as one.

And by the sound of the crowd, they loved it.

Malachi stepped down the stairs and reached for my hand without looking at me. I slid my hand into his, not worrying about how the others would react.

"That was surprisingly simple," I whispered to him as he began walking me into the crowd.

"Yet the entire kingdom demands it happens," he replied with a wink.

Malachi led me through the crowd, and the fae around us congratulated him and bowed to him as we passed.

When we approached the edge of the ballroom, Eli and Lucien were waiting for us. "It's about time your arrogance is made official," Lucien teased before clapping Mal on the shoulder.

He laughed quietly. "Don't worry, brother. I'll refrain from abusing my power against you for the time being."

Adonis's loud voice in the distance caught our attention. "Back off," he growled.

I snapped my eyes in his direction, only to find him standing directly in front of Tessa with his hands in front of him.

Mal was pulling us in their direction before I could react.

"What's going on over here?" Malachi asked as we approached.

I let go of his hand and instantly rushed to Tessa, who was now cowering away from the fae.

Only when I looked at the others, my stomach dropped. Standing before Adonis were the same fae who had antagonized us in the gardens before.

The one I had nearly killed stood before them, only he was completely healed.

His eyes locked on mine, and a grin spread across his face. "Hello again, my queen."

Malachi stepped forward and placed a hand on the fae's chest, pushing him back a step. "Adonis," he said without looking away from the fae. "Tell me what's happening."

"They were messing with Tessa again," was all he said.

I wrapped my arms tighter around my sister and watched as Malachi smiled. "Is that so?" he asked. His black wings flared from beneath his robe. "Am I correct to hear that this is the second time you have disturbed Lady Farrow?"

The fae's jaw clenched.

"My wife dealt with you last time. If I see you talking to either Jade or Tessa again, I'll kill you myself."

Everyone froze, including the small crowd gathering around us. The fae shot me one last look before sliding his eyes over to Tessa. I could have sworn I heard Adonis growl.

"Get out of here," Malachi interrupted. "You're no longer welcome at this celebration."

As soon as they walked away, I grabbed Tessa's shoulders. "Are you alright?" I asked. "Did they hurt you?"

She shook her head. "No, I'm okay. They just wanted to start trouble."

I pulled her into a hug. "I'm sorry, Tessa. Nobody should be bothering you here."

Adonis stepped forward. "They won't bother her again," he hissed.

Tessa pulled away from my grasp and took a long breath. "Get back to your party," she said. "I'll be okay now."

"This is Malachi's party," I reminded her. "Not mine. If you want me to leave and—"

"No," she interrupted. "This is your party, too, Jade." A small smile tugged on her lips. "Let's at least try to have some fun."

And so we did. The air buzzed with joy and excitement of the new king. When the music started again, I pulled Tessa into the crowd and spun her around. At first, she tensed up.

But after a few minutes, her and her beautiful blue dress were spinning through the night.

It wasn't until hours later that I noticed the crowd had nearly dwindled down to half. For a group of fae, leaving a party early was unheard of.

"What's going on?" I asked Serefin as I reached for a cup of water. "Where's everybody going?" Serefin paused for a moment and rolled his shoulders back, as if he were debating whether or not to tell me the truth. "Tell me," I demanded.

"It's the war," he whispered. "Citizens have been leaving all week. They're relocating to the outskirts, where they can stay hidden in case the castle is attacked."

I shook my head. "That's ridiculous. Who will protect them if they leave?"

It didn't make any sense. Citizens were leaving because of the war that approached? What if the outskirts were attacked first? There would be no army to protect them. No walls. No *king*.

"Malachi left the decision up to them," Ser explained. "If they want to leave so badly, they are free to."

A sense of dread built in my stomach. "It's because of me, isn't it? They know I'm the target."

Serefin's dark eyes met mine. "Who cares what they think, Jade? You're Malachi's wife, and you are their new queen. Malachi will protect you along with this kingdom, even if others don't see that."

My eyes found Malachi in the crowd, who was now in deep conversation with a few court members.

"He's giving up a lot for me," I whispered.

Serefin placed a warm hand on my shoulder. "Just as any of us would."

CHAPTER 27
Jade

Days passed quicker than I ever imagined they would. Esther never visited my dreams again, and I never mentioned them. I tried to avoid thinking about her at all, and I stayed far away from the dungeons of the castle.

My life became a mixture of watching over Tessa, training for the upcoming war, and spending as much time as I could with Malachi.

But we could all sense change coming. We could sense the war moving closer and closer.

Our conversations grew quiet. Our training held a sense of desperation with every new movement. Tessa could sense it, too. She stayed hidden in her room more days than not.

Until one day, when life as I knew it ended.

Malachi and I were in his room. We had been spending most of our time there lately, locked away from the chaos of the castle.

A knock came from the door.

"Come in," Malachi ordered.

It was his brother who slowly creaked open the door.

I knew something was wrong the second I laid eyes on Lucien's face. He had *never* looked at me like that.

With such *pity*.

He looked over to Malachi, who stood behind me in the bedroom, and then back to me.

"What?" I asked. "What's wrong?"

Adonis stepped up behind Lucien, and then Eli behind him.

None of them looked me directly in the eye.

The hair on the back of my neck rose.

"Lucien," Malachi spoke. His voice was harsher than I had heard it in a long time. "Say something. What do you need? What's going on?"

"There was an accident," Adonis said. "In the garden. We ran to see what the commotion was, but it was too late."

"What. Happened."

Something was wrong. Something was very, very wrong.

"It's Jade's sister," Adonis said. He bowed his head and stared at the floor.

Panic took over my body. "Is she okay?" I asked as I stepped forward. "Where is she?"

Lucien was the one who stepped up, placing his body in front of me with his hands in front of him. "Jade..."

"Where is she?" I repeated. I couldn't hide the panic creeping into my voice. My mind screamed at me to *go find her. Go find your sister.*

This wasn't happening.

This couldn't be happening.

"Tell me!" I yelled again. The suffocating grip of an invisible hand tightened around my throat.

"She's dead, Jade," Lucien said.

A knife pierced my heart. *Dead.*

No, no, no. That couldn't be right.

"She's...she's dead?" I repeated. My own voice felt foreign. Those words were never supposed to leave my mouth. Not about her. Not about my baby sister.

"What in the Saints happened?" Malachi's voice boomed through the room. His hands came down on my arms, but I could hardly feel them. I didn't care about anyone else.

I needed to see her.

I needed to get to my sister.

"Where?" I asked. "Where is she?"

"There was a fight. We tried to stop it but we were too late, Mal. Tessa was...she was caught in the crossfire."

Malachi's voice thundered so loudly, the frames on the walls vibrated. "Who did it? If someone killed her, you better tell me right now!"

No. This wasn't real. *This wasn't real.*

My body was moving, walking past the brothers who simply slid out of my way as I approached. The gardens. It happened in the gardens.

I had to get to the gardens. I had to get to Tessa.

She wasn't dead. *No, it wasn't possible.*

Tessa was alive. I just had to find her and Malachi could get her to the infirmary and whatever happened, it would all be fine.

It would all be okay. Tessa was *fine.*

I felt Malachi's presence behind me. I walked and walked and walked. At some point, that walk turned into a run.

Before I could even fathom where I was heading, I turned the last corner into the garden.

People were everywhere. No, not people. *Fae.* Standing, mingling, whispering, and then looking at me.

Someone bumped my shoulder. There were too many. Too many faces, too many pairs of wings.

Too many *enemies.*

Malachi must have said something, because the fae in the garden began scattering. Away from the crowd. Away from...

Tessa.

My eyes glued to Tessa, laying in the middle of the walking path next to the bright red roses. I ran to her and dropped to my knees, grabbing ahold of her small shoulders. They felt so cold.

"Tessa?" I asked. I shook her lightly. She seemed so small, much smaller than I remembered. "Tessa, wake up!"

Malachi knelt on the other side of her, but he wasn't looking at Tessa. He watched me with wide eyes.

"Mal, do something!" I yelled. "She's okay, she's okay we just have to get her to–"

"Jade," he cut me off. His voice sounded soft, just like Lucien's. It sounded *sad.* "According to witnesses, it was the same fae who threatened you both in the gardens the other day...he snapped her neck. She's gone, Jade. Your sister is dead."

"No," I insisted. "No!" I looked at her neck. It was...it was twisted into a weird position, her head tilted off to the side. "She's...she's *safe* here. She's supposed to be *safe* here."

Malachi didn't say anything.

My vision blurred with tears. "She's not dead!"

"She's dead, Jade."

A sob ripped through my body. I hadn't felt this hopeless in a very, very long time. For as long as I could remember,

Tessa was my anchor. She was the one thing I had to fight for. Even when I had nothing, even when I had no reason for continuing, I kept fighting. Because my sister needed me.

Tessa saved my life.

Malachi's hands found my face, wiping away the tears that were only replaced with more. How could I have let this happen?

I was her protector. I was the one who took care of her. I was the one who kept her safe.

No, no, no. This could not be real. Tessa couldn't really be dead.

I would wake up in the morning and this would all be one wicked, horrific dream. It was all a nightmare, *yes. That* made sense. That made *perfect* sense.

What didn't make any damned sense was my sister being dead!

I looked back down at her, tears dropping from my chin down to my chest. She was so pale. So lifeless.

I wanted to hug her. I wanted to pull her scrawny little body to mine and hold her until it was all okay, like I had done hundreds of times before. I wanted to go to sleep in our tiny little bed and give her my blanket, too, because hers was never enough to keep her warm in the winter.

I wanted to teach her how to tie a knot, even though she was completely helpless and wasn't getting anywhere with her hunting skills.

I wanted to look her in the eye and tell her I loved her, because Saints, I hadn't done that enough.

"Jade," Malachi's voice interrupted my thoughts. I finally looked at him, but he was staring at something behind me.

When I glanced over my shoulder to see who else was in the garden, another wave of debilitating sorrow hit me.

Father.

"Oh, Tessa," he moaned. He stumbled forward and fell to his knees beside me, grabbing her limp arm. "Tessa, Tessa, Tessa."

I couldn't say anything as I watched the horror. I had hated my father for years, probably more than half my life. I had watched him abandon her time and time again. And time and time again, *I* was the one that stepped in. That told him to sober up, or to get out of the house until he calmed down.

But he was our father. He was *her* father.

Tessa had never looked at him with the same hatred that I did. She was frightened of him at times, and certainly disappointed, but she never hated him.

And I think he knew that.

I wanted to reach out and console him, pat his shoulder as he knelt beside me. But I couldn't.

"What happened?" he said when he looked up. He glanced rapidly between me and Mal. "Tell me what in the Saints happened to my daughter!"

Numb. I felt numb nothingness as Malachi answered, "There was a fight. She was...she was killed."

A shaking sob wrecked through my father. I had only seen this side of him one other time.

But not like this.

My father bent down again, pressing his forehead against hers. Against his cold, dead daughter's skin.

He mumbled things that I couldn't understand, things that I didn't even want to try to understand.

When he looked up after quite some time, it wasn't sorrow that dripped over his features. It was anger.

"You swore to me that she would be safe. That we would be safe here!"

"I know," I breathed.

Shame washed over me. I deserved every bit of it.

"You SWORE to me! She was your sister! Your baby sister!"

"I know."

"She's dead, Jade!"

"I know that!"

The numbness and the adrenaline in my body was replaced in a wash of emotion, filled with anger and shame and despair. I didn't ask for this. I didn't ask for Tessa to die. To be killed by the very fae I risked my life to protect.

Did he not see that? Did he not see that my very reason for living had just been ripped away from me? That without Tessa, I had nothing?

Anger built inside of me, igniting a fire that used my despair to grow hotter and hotter. I should have seen this coming. I should have known she couldn't be protected here. Tessa was too fragile. Too *good*.

"Jade, calm down," Malachi whispered roughly. "You're losing control."

I didn't care. I didn't care if I lost control. I didn't care if this entire damned kingdom burned to the ground.

"Jade!"

Malachi's wings were around my body in two seconds, followed by the uncontrolled flare of my own power.

His massive black wings kept the sudden flash contained.

I wanted to stay there, wrapped away in the darkness.

But when the flash ended, Malachi slowly peeled them back.

And as soon as they parted, I saw the horror on my father's face.

I would have killed him, too. My power would have killed my own father if it weren't for Malachi.

And he knew it.

Hands were on my body, lifting me up and saying something I couldn't focus on. "Let's go. I'm taking you home."

CHAPTER 28
Malachi

"Talk to me, Jade."

It had been hours since we left the garden. I had to drag Jade away from Tessa's body, carrying her up to my bedroom.

And she hadn't said a single word since.

I didn't blame her. I had to hide my own shock when I saw Tessa laying there. She looked so small, so fragile.

So helpless.

Jade knew it, too. She knew that Tessa could have done nothing against a fae if a fae wanted her dead. It was a very similar position that Jade was in not too long ago.

Now, Jade had other problems.

"Just let me know that you'll be okay," I pushed. I sat next to her on the bed. She stared at the dark ceiling, although her eyes had been glazed over for the last hour. She wasn't in there. She was a hollow void, completely numb to any emotion.

I had felt similar at many times in my life. I knew Jade had, too.

Raw. Emotionless. Empty.

I brushed a piece of hair off her forehead. It wasn't until my skin made contact with hers that she blinked twice and her eyes met mine. "I can't do this," she admitted. "I can't do this, Mal. I can't be this person."

I caressed her cheek. "You can, Jade."

She shook her head, tears filling that emptiness in her eyes. "She was my reason for living, Mal. You don't understand. Without her, I have..."

I held her face gently. "You have everything, Jade. Do you hear me? You have Adeline. You have Serefin. You have entire kingdoms of people counting on you. You are needed, Jade. And you are loved. By a whole lot of people now, not just Tessa. The *world* needs you."

I knew my words were void. She wouldn't care. She wouldn't even have the capacity of caring about anything other than her dead sister right now.

But with war on the horizon, I had to try.

Jade needed to hang on. She needed to dig deep, into that small, hidden corner of perseverance that only came out in situations like this. In situations where you didn't want to continue. Didn't want to live.

But you had no choice.

Because someone counted on you. Someone would miss you.

Saints.

I had choked back those words for too long.

I leaned forward and displaced my forehead against Jade's. She needed to hear me when I said this. She needed to feel how I felt.

"I love you, Jade," I whispered. Jade's eyes closed. "I love you, and I know you are hurting. And I would trade places with you in a heartbeat, Jade, because it *kills* me to see you in pain. It kills me to see you like this. You are my everything, Jade. You *deserve* everything. And I know you don't care about what I have to say right now. I know you're empty and numb and contemplating how the *Saints* you'll continue, but you *have* to know this—I love you deeply, Jade. *Insatiably.* How I lived so many years without you, I have no clue. But you walked into my life when I had given up, and you pulled me back from the ledge when I only wanted to jump. So that's what I'm going to do to you now, Jade. I'm pulling you back from that ledge. Because I'm *selfish* and I *don't want* to go on without you. So I'll let you sleep this off, but come morning, I'll be here. And I'll be here the next day, and the next day. Because *I can't live* without you."

I stayed there for a moment, half-in awe at the words I had just spoken, before I moved to stand. If she wanted alone time, I would give it to her. No matter how badly I wanted to do just the opposite.

"Wait," her frail voice stopped me in my tracks. "Thank you, Malachi."

I turned around and grabbed her outstretched hand. The chill of her skin shocked me. "For what?"

Tears spilled down both of her cheeks. "You weren't the only one that needed to be pulled back from that ledge."

Later that night, while Jade was fast asleep next to me, I snuck out of the room.

I killed all five of the fae that were seen messing with Tessa.

And I strung each of their dead bodies from ropes in the dining hall.

CHAPTER 29

Jade

There were many times in my life that I wished my sister were dead. It would have been easier without her. Thinking that now sounded cruel, but it was true. At times, Tessa could be the most clueless human alive. Saints, all of those years watching me and I don't think she ever learned to hunt.

She had tried, of course. And failed. Many, many times. Part of me thought she was so bad at it on purpose, so that she would never have to be relied on like I was.

I smiled at the memory. If that were the case, she was smarter than I gave her credit for.

Malachi slept next to me. I listened to the sound of his deep, calming breaths.

I hadn't slept much at all. Every time I closed my eyes, I saw her. And then I saw her mangled, twisted neck laying on the pavement of the garden.

And I saw my father screaming over her dead body.

I tried not to care about him. I tried not to think about where he had gone after Malachi ripped me away. Saints, part of me wished he would just go get drunk. Anything to escape from the pain.

Anything.

Malachi's wings tucked around us on the bed. Somehow, I felt safer near him. My entire life had just been ripped away from me, but when I was near him...

I wasn't entirely lost.

He had gotten up just hours before, thinking I was asleep. I knew he was going to avenge Tessa's death. I knew he wouldn't let something so vile go on in his own kingdom.

And I also knew that the guilt was eating at him. The guilt that he didn't keep her safe.

Same as me.

Except he wasn't the one to blame. I was.

Malachi shifted awake next to me, slowly blinking his eyes open before he realized I was already awake.

He sat up instantly, half-jumping out of the bed.

"I'll get you something to eat."

"No. I'm coming with you," I insisted. "I'm not going to hide my face around here. I want everyone to see me. To see that I'm not just going to roll over."

"You can give it a day, Jade, you don't–"

"I'm coming, and that's final."

Malachi stared at me for a second longer before nodding. "Okay," he said. "But if you're uncomfortable for even a second, we're leaving. I have a private dining room for a reason, you know."

I didn't care. War approached us. I was not going to let my enemies within this castle think they had won.

For Tessa. I would do this for Tessa.

I quickly got dressed. My hair fell in loose waves, and I

didn't even try to maintain the chaos of it. My arms were heavy, much heavier than they were yesterday. Everything was heavy.

"Let me," Mal said after he saw me struggling to braid it.

He came up behind me, his presence instantly electrifying my body. My eyes were raw, red, and glassy. I didn't care. Hiding it was pointless. This was how a grieving human looked.

"You know how to braid?" I asked.

Malachi pulled all of my hair behind my back, his fingers brushing the sides of my neck when he did. "How hard can it be?" he whispered.

I smiled. It felt wrong, but I let it happen. "You're awfully old to be a man who doesn't know how to braid."

He struggled to split my hair into three uneven sections. "I am a man of many talents, my dear wife," he started. His words sent a chill down my spine. "But braiding long, beautiful hair is not one of them. Yet."

I spent the next few minutes in silence, watching him in the mirror as he worked, with utter focus, on braiding my waist-length locks.

If I hadn't been in love with him before, I certainly would be now.

"Tessa was beginning to warm up to you, you know," I said.

Mal looked up in shock, either because of what I said or because he wasn't expecting me to be talking about her. "Really?"

I nodded. "I think Adonis actually made a good impression too, believe it or not."

Malachi smiled this time. "That's one that I'll believe when I see."

Our smiles both dropped then, because we would never see that. We would never see Tessa smile again. Would never hear her talk.

Malachi finished my braid and placed both of his hands on my shoulders. They felt no heavier than the weight that already lay there.

I leaned my head back onto his shoulder and closed my eyes.

Tears threatened my eyes. I let them come. If I tried to hold back every tear today, I wouldn't survive.

Malachi leaned his head on mine. A silent agreement, an unspoken promise. I wouldn't be going through this alone. I wouldn't have to carry this burden by myself.

"Your strength is inspiring, my queen," he whispered before pressing his lips to my temple. "We'll get through this together."

I didn't speak. I just took a few long breaths, taking in Malachi's presence behind me, before opening my eyes again and stepping toward the door. "It's now or never," I said, choking down the emotion that threatened to erupt. "Let's show those bastards they can't take me down that easily."

When Malachi didn't follow, I turned to look at him. The amount of utter pride in his expression was almost enough to drop me to my knees.

"I know you don't feel like you belong here all of the time," he spoke. "But you are the best queen these fae have ever known."

He grabbed my hand and we walked to the dining hall in silence.

Five minutes later, I was staring at five dead bodies.

Hanging from the ceiling of the dining hall.

The roaring conversations in the room around me seemed to halt. Blurs of wings and colors passed by as my vision locked in.

Nobody seemed to pay any attention to them. The entire dining hall was packed full of citizens, silently going about their business and eating their breakfast.

"I assume this was your doing?" I asked Mal.

His eyes darkened as he stared at the corpses. "This crime was not going to go unpunished."

There might have been a younger version of me that would have been mortified by the image in front of me. Blood continued to drip on the floor from each of their impaled bodies.

But today? A bright ball of satisfaction lit up in my stomach.

They had paid with their lives. By Malachi's hand.

And I knew more than anyone that Malachi was sending a message with this act.

I turned my attention away from the bodies and back to the room full of fae. "Everyone's staring at us," I whispered to Mal.

"Don't worry," he assured. "That's nothing new."

We walked to the head table of the dining hall, the one that was reserved for Malachi.

Even though he rarely ate here.

Servants greeted us as soon as we sat down, our backs to the wall with those corpses hanging in my direct line of sight.

"My queen," one servant asked me. "We have fresh fruit, picked just this morning from our fields. Absolutely divine."

She set a massive bowl in front of me with an assortment of colorful fruits.

I nodded my thanks, but I didn't miss the sparkle of pity in her eye.

At least the servants cared.

Malachi's tension spread to me as we sat there, but his chin didn't drop an inch. He looked everyone in the eye as they stared at us.

Part of me wanted to look away. The other part of me welled with a familiar pride that reminded me of the way he had looked at me earlier.

My king.

I was completely thrown off guard when a body slammed into mine from the side, wrapping me in a tight hug.

Adeline.

"Saints, Jade. I'm so, so terribly sorry. I've been thinking about you nonstop and I wanted to come say hi but I didn't want to bug you and–"

"I'm okay, Adeline," I said, awkwardly trying to hug her back from where I sat

"Get off of her, Adeline," Mal warned from his chair beside me.

Adeline dragged a wooden chair next to me, so close that our legs were touching. "Tell me," she started. Her eyes filled with so much worry that I truly didn't know how to respond. "How are you?"

"I'm okay," I responded. The words were uncomfortably true.

She glanced at the hanging corpses, and I watched as her nostrils flared in disgust. "They deserve to rot for what they did," she muttered.

"They will," I whispered. A comforting wave of power fell over my senses. "I have a feeling everyone who has ever wronged me will get their turn very, very soon."

Adeline's eyes snapped to mine. Something dark lingered in her gaze. Something dark and...familiar. Something hungry. "I know you'll rip them to shreds, Jade," she said. Her hand came up to tug on my messy braid. "Just don't feel guilty about it," she said.

"About what?"

Adeline's eyes darkened. It was rare for me to see her in this spirit. "About taking over the world and ending anyone in your way," she said. "And liking it."

Before I could even process what she had just said, Adeline was leaving the table.

"Well," Mal cleared his throat. "I'm glad to know she hasn't completely lost her mind."

My heart warmed. Adeline was a cheerful, optimistic source of light in Rewyth. But ever since the festival in Trithen, I saw who she really was.

Adeline chose to be that bright light. She had overcome the impossible and survived a life around power hungry, abusive men. Adeline had risen from the ashes, and she was here to create her own destiny now. After so much of her own life had been stripped from her, she chose light.

I admired that about her. That she could have so much taken away and still choose to see the good.

I couldn't say I particularly felt the same.

"Jade?" Malachi's voice pulled me from my trance. "Did you hear me?"

"No," I stuttered. "Sorry. Can you say it again?"

Mal smiled, but it dripped in concern. "I said you better hurry up and eat before your food gets cold."

"Right," I agreed, hurrying to pick up my fork. "Sorry, I was just a little distracted."

"You have nothing to apologize for," he said.

I ate for a few minutes. Swallowing each bite was a nearly impossible task, but there were too many prying eyes watching me. Too many people looking for a weakness to exploit.

The flavor of the food, the same flavor that I had been disgustingly astonished with when I had first tasted it, was now nothing but bland mush.

It wasn't until Lucien and Adonis slid into the two seats in front of us that I really felt my senses light up.

"What are you doing?" Mal asked, slightly bored.

"You shouldn't be out here," Lucien started. "It's not safe."

"Not safe?" Mal laughed beside me. "And why is that?"

Adonis and Lucien exchanged a glance. "There are a few who aren't thrilled about their friends dripping blood on our breakfast plates."

The low murmurs of conversations around us halted. The only thing I cared about now was Malachi sitting next to me. He looked calm, but I could feel the thrill of power inside of me reacting to his.

Waiting.

"Tell me who," Mal shrugged. "Who's unhappy with the justice their king decides to bestow upon them?"

Lucien's eyes glanced over in my direction, only for a split second, before returning to Mal. "Many people, brother."

When Mal laughed this time, he didn't hold anything back.

"What's funny?" Adonis asked.

"What?" Mal asked. "You don't find this funny?"

"This is serious," Lucien hissed, leaning across the table and lowering his voice. "We're on the brink of war, brother. We can't have an uprising."

"Who?" It took me two seconds to realize that it was me who asked.

All eyes turned to mine. "What?" Mal questioned.

"Who was it that was concerned? You said many, so point to a few." *Shut up, shut up, shut up.*

I couldn't stop, though. It was like another force controlled me, controlled my words.

"There are too many to point to," Adonis answered.

"I'm sure you can point to one. Two, at the most. Don't be shy."

Adonis's forehead wrinkled. When I glanced at Mal, he just stared expectantly at his brothers. He, too, waited for an answer.

Time ticked by.

The utter void of emotionlessness inside of me churned, producing a low burn of anger and hatred and vile that crept–like fire–into the rest of my body. It started in my stomach, burning there slowly until it spread up my torso, into my chest. My breath got heavier. Thicker. More labored.

An emotion crept into that fire. More than one emotion, actually.

I couldn't tell. But I did know one thing—I wanted answers.

And I would not be denied.

I stood up from my chair and placed my hands on the wooden table in front of me. I wasn't angry at Adonis, no. Not even at Lucien, who had been the target of my anger on more than one occasion. My eyes scanned the room around me.

Some friends. Some foes. Mostly strangers.

Yet somehow, when my eyes met the ones that lingered upon me, powerlessness began to creep up my spine, biting and clawing its way back up.

That was what bothered me the most. I may have been broken. I may have been kicked and beaten and whipped into submission, both figuratively and literally. But I was still alive. Even when death welcomed me with open and cold arms, I had stepped forward.

And that made me far from powerless.

Mal's brothers stared at me with wide eyes, but I continued anyway.

"It's been brought to my attention that some of you may have a problem with the way my husband has chosen to punish our enemies," I spoke with strength. The chatter in the room halted, the air was all but sucked out.

Nothing. No answer. No admission.

Interesting.

Malachi stood next to me, either because he wanted to protect me or because he felt the pull of my power.

I felt it, too. That burning sensation in my chest grew and grew. "Nobody?" I asked.

A young male stepped forward. His silver wings tucked behind his shoulder blades. "They were our friends," he spoke. The words alone were innocent, but the malice that laced them sounded anything but.

"They killed my sister."

A male beside him laughed.

The power inside of me grew hotter.

Mal brushed his fingertips across my lower back. Enough for me to know he was there if I needed him, but light enough to tell me I had permission.

I lifted a palm from the wooden table, just in time, and a ball of white-hot power skidded through the dining hall, bursting just before the young fae's feet. He jumped in fear.

Others screamed.

"What?" I asked, lifting an eyebrow. "Something wrong?"

I stepped around the table and descended the few steps to the rest of the dining hall. Heading straight toward the fae who laughed.

Mal trailed my every step, but stayed silent.

"What–what are you doing?" he asked as I approached.

I held my hands out in front of me and let my power express itself again.

Others were staring now, half in horror and half in pure curiosity. I stared back, daring anyone to push me.

"They killed my sister," I said again. "And they paid with their lives. Now, lucky for you all, I only had one sister. But unlucky for you all, I'm feeling particularly fed up with being walked on in my own kingdom."

I dropped my hands and the power erupted around us. Everyone ducked to avoid the small blast—everyone but Malachi and me.

When everyone looked back up again, it was Malachi and I standing in the center of the dining hall.

"A move against my wife is a move against this kingdom," Malachi's voice boomed. "If anyone has a problem with the way that I punish traitors to the crown, it won't be me you answer to. It will be my wife."

"Let's get out of here," I said. I slid my hand into Malachi's and walked toward the dining room entrance.

I never wanted power. But in those moments where I would have given anything for it all to be over, I found myself wishing I had a single shred of strength.

Today, it was strength alone that pulled me out of bed. And strength alone forced me to continue.

CHAPTER 30
Malachi

Jade had no idea what type of men would be waiting for her outside of the castle. She had insisted that Ser and I take her out to the troops. It was only fair, considering they were fighting for *her* life.

Her black boots ground the dirt beneath us. Ser and I followed a few footsteps behind, but my eyes didn't leave her for a single second.

Ser and I had been coming out here daily, training these men and getting to know them. Not all of them were our friends, but right now, they were our allies. That mattered more than friendship.

But to Jade, it was all the same.

She was pushing herself. I could see it in her eyes. I would catch her staring into the distance, smiling to herself with her eyes glossed over. Each time, I wanted to ask her what she was thinking about. What memory was so precious that she was reliving it now.

But those were her memories, sacred between her and her

sister. If she needed to escape into those memories, into those few moments of peace, then I would let her.

And I wouldn't interrupt.

Men greeted Ser and I as we entered the field of campsites. I noted the way they each either nodded their heads in Jade's direction or ignored her entirely.

Both were better than confronting her, in my eyes.

"These men are comfortable enough out here?" Jade asked without looking at me. She was too busy observing the makeshift housing.

"Comfortable enough," Ser answered. "We have given every possible resource to housing these men. They would much rather sleep under the stars than crammed into the old servants' quarters of the castle."

Jade smiled to herself again. "I can't blame them. The stars are beautiful."

My heart twisted. Jade admired the stars because they were free. That was something Jade had never experienced herself.

Would she ever?

Jade continued to walk through the masses, assessing every man who was preparing to give his life for our cause.

Until Carlyle approached. "Lady Weyland," he bent at the waist in greeting. "It's a pleasure seeing you again."

Jade bowed her own head in greeting. "You look well," she responded. I stepped to the side of her.

"Don't tell him that," I teased, placing a hand on her lower back. "It'll go straight to his head." Carlyle smiled, but the typical light in his eyes was gone. Replaced by something darker. "What's going on?"

Carlyle glanced around us and motioned to follow him

back into the dining hall. Once inside, he leaned forward and whispered, "Our scouts have sent word. War is coming. Now."

"Now?" Jade asked. "As in, today?"

"Yes, my queen. We need to get everyone ready for an attack from the Paragon."

"How many of them?" I asked.

Carlyle took a deep breath before answering, "That depends on what you're asking. If you're asking how many deadlings, I'd say one to two hundred. If you're asking how many soldiers, it looks to be around a thousand men."

Hundreds of deadlings. Thousands of men. "Saints."

"What do we do?" Jade asked.

My body buzzed with adrenaline. This was it. Everything we had prepared for was happening. "Go find Adeline and tell her what's happening," I said. "I'm going to take Serefin and alert the troops."

"What about everyone else?" she asked, referencing the men around us. "What do we tell them?"

Carlyle stepped backward and spoke to the entire dining hall, "All able-bodied men—please make your way out to the front gates. Nothing to worry about, just a precaution." Would I ever be able to lie that easily to my own people? To tell them that everything was fine on the verge of war?

Jade tugged my hand. "What will you do?"

"Go," I urged, the room now slowly brewing chaos with Carlyle's announcement. "I'll come find you."

She hesitated, just for a second. Was she afraid? Was she regretting ever taking my side? She had to know that everyone in this kingdom was here to protect her by now.

But she was still a human...

After one more second, she let go of my hand and lost herself in the sea of fae.

She would be fine. She would find Adeline and Adeline would know what to do, Adeline would know to hide her away in the dungeons until I came for them both.

I hoped to the Saints that they actually listened to me.

CHAPTER 31
Jade

"Okay," Adeline said for the tenth time. "Okay, okay."

"Do you have a plan for this type of thing?" I asked.

"Yes, yes there's a plan. Malachi gave me strict instructions."

"What did he tell you?"

Adeline's mind went somewhere else, digging for the instructions that Mal had given her. Her eyes were wide with panic, but she fought to stay calm. "The dungeons!" she snapped back to the present time. In two seconds, she transformed from a frazzled girl to a fae on a mission. She grabbed my wrist and began pulling me to her bedroom door "Let's go."

I pulled against her, but her fae strength was no match for me. "What?"

"We have to stay in the dungeons until Malachi comes to get us"

"Are you kidding? We'll be sitting ducks down there!"

"It's the safest place for us," she argued. "The chances of anyone making it far enough to find us in there are slim."

My mind spun in circles. I wasn't helpless. I wasn't about to sit in the dungeon and wait for the Paragon to find me. I was to blame for this attack. I was to blame for the Paragon coming here.

I owed it to Mal to fight, even if he wanted me to hide.

But there was another person who could help us. Who could help me.

And in order to find her, I had to get to the dungeons.

"Fine," I said. "Let's go."

I let Adeline drag me under the castle. I had never seen the halls so busy, bustling with both fae men and women shuffling in opposite directions. The men rushed outside, and the women ran in a panic.

A wave of pity fell over me. They were fae, they were powerful. I had spent my entire life thinking they were indestructible. But at last, they too had something to fear. They too could be helpless against their opponents.

When we got to the entrance of the dungeons, the guards were waiting for us. "Malachi's orders," Adeline spoke. "The castle is being attacked. Today."

The guard's face didn't change as he stepped aside, letting us in. "Thank you," Adeline muttered, and then she was pulling me into the dark underground tunnels.

I followed silently behind her until we got to the fork in the long halls. Esther was to the right. But Adeline began pulling me left. "Stop," I halted. "Adeline, wait."

She stopped and spun to face me. "What?"

"Esther is this way," I pointed to the right. "We have to tell her what's going on. She can help us, Adeline."

"No way," she argued. "Mal will kill us if we even speak to her."

"Mal can't see past his anger. Esther is a witch, and we're being attacked by the Paragon. We can't just leave her chained down here Adeline, that makes no sense!"

Her nostrils flared as she debated the options. I knew she would see my side. Esther might be the only person in this entire kingdom with the knowledge to fight another witch, and if what I had heard about the Paragon so far was true, they would bring witches with them to fight.

Malachi was strong. But could he defeat them all?

"If we get caught," she started, "I'm blaming you."

"I'm totally fine with that." I turned on my heels and began rushing toward Esther's cell. It had been so long since I had been down here last. I hadn't realized just how long these halls really were.

We walked and walked and walked. "Are you sure it's this way?" Adeline asked me. "These tunnels really creep me out."

My senses tingled with every step. We were close. We had to be. "I think it's—"

"I knew you would be coming for me," Esther's voice muttered through the halls. Adeline and I followed that voice, rounding one last corner and finding Esther in her cell.

"You can see the future now?" I asked.

Esther was sitting in that same dark corner, yet she looked ten years older.

"Did you forget I am a witch, child?"

"Jade didn't forget anything," Adeline stepped in. "That's why we're here."

"Is that so?" Esther asked. She tried to shift herself on the ground, but a violent coughing fit stopped her. I looked away. "Need one more look before I finally die?"

"It's time," I said. "The Paragon will attack before night-fall. You told me you would help."

"Ah, so now you've finally decided you need me. Is that it?"

"You can either sit here and rot," I said, "or you can help your son win this war."

She was silent for a few moments. "Does he know you're here?"

"Does that make a difference?"

"It does," she said, "because I know my son will never want me to fight beside him again. If I show my face outside of these dungeons..."

"He wants your help," I interrupted. "He just doesn't know if he can trust you."

Esther smiled; her once perfectly white teeth were now beginning to rot. "I tried to kill him. I would have killed you, too. Although that would have been a mercy compared to what the Paragon will do with you."

"You really feel no remorse? You could have lived a long, happy life knowing that you murdered your own son?" Adeline spat.

Esther's face hardened. "I've lived a lot longer than the both of you combined. You have no idea what it takes to live a long, happy life."

"Don't speak down to me," Adeline said. "I know plenty. I am not a witch, but I know how to be happy. And turning on those who trust you is not going to help you. Especially since you failed in your efforts to take the power from the peacemaker."

I stayed silent. Hearing Adeline speak with so much passion was both inspiring and bone-chilling.

"Look," I interrupted. "You can fight this all you want. You can stay down here and rot and think that you're better than all of us because of it. Or you can get over your self-right-eousness and try to make it up to Malachi. Fight beside him. Fight for him. Redeem yourself."

"Redeem myself," she mumbled. Her hands began rubbing at her chained wrists. "I'm afraid I lost that chance a long time ago."

"You won't even try?" I asked.

"I'm just one person. Even if I tried to help, I'm too weak now. I'll have no magic."

"You'll find a way," I argued. She had enough magic to enter my dream the other night. That meant something. "If it's important enough, you'll try."

Seconds felt like hours. Adeline and I stood at the entrance of the cell, waiting for her answer. Waiting for a sign of hope.

It was a dangerous thing, counting on someone else. I prayed to the Saints that this wasn't a massive mistake.

"Okay," she finally said. "If you let me out, I'll fight by my son's side. I'll do what I can, I'll talk to the Paragon. But I can't promise you anything."

I sighed in relief.

"We just have to get you out of these chains..."

"Please," Adeline shrugged, pulling a small pin from her long hair. "I've got this."

She approached Esther and knelt by her side, gently picking the cuffs on her wrists with the pin.

In a few seconds, the chains clattered to the ground. "Can you stand?"

"Of course, I can stand. I'm not dead yet." She attempted to move to her feet, but struggled with every movement.

Saints. Maybe she wouldn't be any help to us after all.

Adeline eventually grabbed her arm to help her up. "You just need to get out of these dungeons. You'll feel much better once you see the sun."

Esther stayed silent. Adeline didn't let go of her as she took one step. And then another.

"The next challenge will be getting past the guard."

"Well how did you two sneak in here?" Esther mumbled. "I assume if you got yourselves past them once, you can do it again."

"With a prisoner? Sure, sounds easy."

My blood was pounding in my ears. Even in the chill of the tunnels, a bead of sweat ran down my spine.

If this didn't work, I would be in trouble.

And Malachi would be pissed.

"Let me do the talking," Adeline said as we approached the entrance. "Stay back."

Adeline let go of Esther, and I had to grab ahold of Esther's arm to ensure she could still stand.

To my surprise, Esther didn't fight it.

We stayed back while Adeline trotted forward to speak with the guard.

I strained to hear what they were saying.

"I'm sorry about your sister," Esther whispered to me.

I snapped my attention to her. "What?"

"Your sister, Tessa. I'm sorry that she died."

If my heart hadn't already been pounding as fast as possible, I was sure it would have started. "How do you know about that?"

"I have many gifts, child," she spoke. "I sensed it as soon as it happened."

Stay focused, I thought. I couldn't get distracted. I couldn't let Tessa infiltrate my thoughts.

"At least those bastards got what they deserved," she said when I didn't speak.

"Yes," I agreed. My teeth were grinding so hard my jaw ached. "They did. And I intend on making anyone who lifts a finger against me pay."

Esther laughed quietly. "I have no doubt about that, child. You are only just beginning to learn how powerful you truly are."

I wanted to ask her more, but Adeline was trotting back in our direction. "What happened?" I asked.

Her face lit up. "He left. I told him Malachi would need his help, and that it was his duty to protect his king. Honestly, that was much easier than it should have been. We should restaff."

"Maybe the Saints are on our side," I stated. "Let's go."

"Where are we going?" Esther muttered. "What's the big plan?"

CHAPTER 32

Malachi

I felt them before I heard them. Hundreds of deadlings tumbling over one another, catastrophically plummeting their dead, decaying bodies toward the kingdom.

Toward *my* kingdom.

My power wouldn't work against them, but I prepared myself for that. I didn't need my power to drop these monsters to the ground.

They would all die, just like they did the last time they came for us.

Every single one of them would die.

"You shouldn't be out here," Serefin spoke when he found me. "Go inside. You'll be the first target they aim for."

"There's no way I'm letting my own soldiers fight this battle without me."

"There is, brother," Serefin sheathed his sword and grabbed me by both of the shoulders. His eyes were frantic as they scanned my face. "I know you want to fight with us. I know that more than anything. But you're no longer a prince.

You are our *king*. We need you alive more than we need you fighting beside us on this battlefield."

My first instinct was to shrug him away and tell him he was wrong. But that slightly desperate look in his eyes made me pause. I had only seen Serefin desperate like this a handful of other times.

I needed to stay alive, yes, but I also had no plans of dying. "I can't sit inside the castle while you all fight the war that I brought on, Serefin. I can help."

"Then help. But only when you can. You can't do anything against the deadlings that the hundreds of men you brought here to fight can't already do. We have the men. We have the weapons. Go inside and wait for the real fighting to begin."

"You want me to wait for the Paragon to arrive?"

Serefin nodded. "That's when we'll need you, Mal. And you sure as shit better still be alive."

I shook my head. "If you need me–"

"We won't need you, Mal. As much as I would love to fight by your side, we have more weapons and soldiers than anyone. We have traps set up in the forest and we have blocked the castle doors. Nobody's getting past that gate."

He was right. This was no surprise attack. We had spent weeks preparing the land around us, reinforcing every weak spot and creating as many obstacles as we could for potential attackers.

"Fine," I said. "But at the first sign of trouble, I'm coming to help."

He seemed to relax a little then, finally letting my words sink in. If it meant this much that I would stay out of sight for a while, I would oblige.

E M I L Y   B L A C K W O O D

"Now go find your sister and Jade," Serefin suggested. "Because we both know there's no way they took your orders to stay put."

I laughed before turning away from the battlefield.

The soldiers I passed on my way inside did not look the least bit concerned.

Determined. Ready. Preparing their weapons and moving their bodies.

Those were the soldiers I trained. Those were the soldiers I could trust.

Jade could trust them, too. Trust them to protect her with their lives. Because that's exactly what we were all doing here today, laying down our lives to protect Jade's.

I walked through the front doors of the castle just before my men boarded them closed. Serefin was right. The odds of her and Adeline doing what they were told and staying hidden in the dungeons were low.

I made my way toward Adeline's bedroom. It was a start.

The heels of my boots clicked on the stone floor as I walked. The castle was now barren, emptied out and turned down as if nobody lived here at all. The servants would be hiding in the tunnels, along with the few women and children that lived here.

I hated that there was no better option. If anything were to go wrong, everyone would be sitting ducks in here.

Which only increased the pure desperation I felt to win this battle. To crush our enemies.

"King Malachi," a strange voice called after me. I spun around in the darkening hallway to find none other than Jade's father walking after me.

His clothes were worn and ripped. Saints, had the maids

not given him enough changes of clothing? He walked slowly, but did not stumble. His usual blood-rimmed eyes seemed clear now. Focused.

On me.

"What are you doing out here?" I asked. "You should be hiding away. The castle is going to be attacked soon. You'll be safe in your rooms."

He held his hands up to stop me from talking. Not in a disrespectful way, though. I could practically feel the desperation of this man boiling off of him.

"I can't," he said.

"Can't what?"

"I can't hide while your enemies come for my daughter. Let me help you."

Both shock and disbelief washed over me. If only Jade could see this now. Would she laugh in his face? Or give the man a chance?

Surely, in a fight against a fae, this man would lose. Not only was he human, he was barely alive. A strong gust of wind would knock him off his feet.

If he stayed away from the liquor that long.

"I understand you want to help," I started with caution, "but I can guarantee you we have this covered."

I began turning back toward Adeline's bedroom when he closed the distance between us and grabbed ahold of my arm.

"Please," he begged. "I lost one daughter. I know I do not deserve this. I know you have no reason to trust me. But...I have to do something. Give me a sword and I'll fight. I'll protect the women and children. Anything."

I could have snapped his neck right there for laying a hand on his king.

Jade's father deserved no mercy. No kindness.

But if he wanted to lose his life fighting for his daughter, who was I to stop him?

"Okay," I admitted. "The front door has been nailed shut already. Follow this hall to the servant's entrance, and let them know I sent you. They'll give you a weapon there."

A flicker of something lit up his dark eyes. "Thank you," he said, bowing his head and holding his hands together. "Thank you, Malachi. You will not regret this."

"No, I won't," I said. "But you might."

I watched as Jade's father half-ran down the hallway, toward the servants' entrance of the castle and outside to face the battlefield.

Finding Jade was even more important after whatever just happened.

When I got to Adeline's bedroom, though, it was empty.

Every room in the entire hallway seemed to be empty.

My mind was spinning, heart pounding in my chest.

The dungeons. They must have actually listened to me and gone to the dungeons.

My feet carried me there until her pitch-black hair came into view. I stopped in my tracks.

"I hope this is some sort of twisted joke," I said. All three of them froze at the sound of my voice, including Adeline who let out a small scream.

"Malachi!" she stuttered. "We were just—"

"Save it. Whatever crazy plan you three thought up to get Esther out of here, it isn't going to happen."

"Esther can help us, Mal," Jade said. "You have to understand that."

"What I understand is the fact that you two thought

letting a traitor free during a war was a good idea. But I suppose it was my fault for leaving you two unattended. My bad. It won't be happening again."

I stepped forward to grab ahold of Esther's arm, but Jade placed a hand on my chest to stop me. "Listen to me," she whispered, loud enough for only me to hear. "This war is happening because of me. *All* of this is because of me. This is a mess that I created, Mal. If I didn't do everything I could to prevent mass casualties in my own kingdom..."

Her voice cracked as she spoke. I placed a hand on top of hers, holding it to my chest.

"This is war, Jade," I explained. "Men have gone to war over *far* less. You don't need to feel bad for anything, and you certainly don't need to feel responsible. But I know what I'm doing. If I thought for even a second that Esther could help us win this battle, I would use her. But she can't."

"Why not?" she asked. Her deep, endless eyes searched mine. "She'll rot in that dungeon anyway, Mal. Give her a chance. If anything, let her prove herself to you."

Jade really didn't see it. She didn't see that my mother was just another wicked creature who would do and say anything necessary to achieve what they wanted. If Adeline and Jade were helping her out now, it wasn't so she could fight on my behalf in battle.

I would be surprised if the woman didn't try to kill me again.

But these two didn't see that. They saw an old woman on her deathbed. They saw a witch with no way out.

"Can you even stand on your own?" I asked over Jade's head. "How are you supposed to fight in battle?"

"I have other uses than fighting in battle, son. I know you

don't trust me. Neither of you do. But this is the end of the road for me. I've lived my life. I've had my chance. I was wrong to betray you, son. I know that now. If you let me help your soldiers in battle with whatever magic I may still possess, you will not regret it."

"What I will regret is letting you free to betray my people again."

Something like pain crossed Esther's face. "The way I see it, you have nothing to lose."

Saints. She was certainly right about that. Esther had grown weak in the dungeons. She was not the witch she was before.

"Fine," I said after a few seconds. "But if you even think about betraying me, I won't capture you as a prisoner. I'll kill you right there. I don't care how useful you claim to be to Jade and I."

Esther nodded in gratitude. "Adeline, show Esther where to go. Then come back here immediately."

"You got it," she muttered. I waited until Adeline and Esther were far enough away before grabbing ahold of Jade's arm.

"Ow!" she yelped. "What are you doing?"

"What you should have been doing this entire time. Hiding you."

I began dragging her back toward the entrance of the dungeons. "Malachi, stop!" she yelled. She tried to dig her heels into the ground beneath her, but she wasn't strong enough to stop me from pulling her along with me.

"You're too valuable, Jade. Keeping you alive is the number one priority. Not only for me. For everyone on that damn battlefield right now."

"I'm not useless! My power can help them all!"

"It's too risky."

"You're not the one who decides that, Malachi!" she brought her free hand up and slapped me across the face.

Hard.

I let her go and she stumbled backward, hands covering her mouth. *Did she really just hit me?*

"Saints," she muttered. "Mal, I'm sorry. I wasn't thinking I just wanted you to–"

"It's fine," I said, unable to keep the amusement from my voice. "And you're right. I'm not the one who decides that, Jade."

I stepped forward and placed my hands on either side of her face, forcing her to look up at me. "I want you to be free. I want nothing more than for you to do whatever the Saints you want to do in this life. But you can't do that if you're dead, Jade. So please, if you have ever listened to me, I *need* you to do this. I need you to stay safe."

"They're your soldiers, Mal! If I can help them, even a few of them, by using my powers while also staying hidden, what's to stop us?"

I opened my mouth to reply, but was cut off by the booming sensation of a cannon hitting the grounds nearby.

Her eyes widened. "What was that?"

My blood ran cold. "They're here."

CHAPTER 33
Jade

"Where are we going now?" I asked. Something I said must have hit home with Malachi, because he was no longer dragging me into the depths of the dungeons to hide away for the entire battle.

We were heading somewhere else.

"You were right," he said. He pulled me down the hallways of the castle in a direction I had never been before. "These are my people, but they are also yours. We shouldn't just leave them undefended when we have power that can help them."

"Wow. Malachi Weyland admitting I'm right? Our kingdom might be falling, after all."

"Not the time for jokes, Jade," he sneered, but I saw the way he hid his smile.

Mal pulled me into a small wooden doorway that we both had to duck to get inside of. Once we were in, I could see a spiral staircase leading upward.

"We're going up?" I asked.

"To the roof," he answered. He led the way, taking step

after step with his black wings tucked in tight so they would fit in the small corridor.

"Sounds much better than hiding in dungeons," I replied.

I tried to keep my voice calm, but the closer we got to the roof, the louder the shouts and screams from the battlefield became. "Deadlings?" I asked.

"They'll attack first with deadlings," Mal answered. Holding onto his hand was enough to keep me sane. He had done this before. Saints, he was practically a professional at battle.

I knew nothing.

"They'll try to weaken our armies. It won't work, though. Deadlings may have caught us off guard the last time, but we prepared for this."

"How are they even controlling them? I thought deadlings had a mind of their own?"

"It has to be the Paragon. Either a witch or a fae who has the power to control others. That's the only explanation."

He let go of my hand to pull himself through a small hole at the end of the staircase.

Once he was through, he reached down to help me up.

Saints. We really were on top of the castle.

The flat roof allowed us to maneuver easily, and a small ledge kept us hidden from the battlefield.

The smell of rotting flesh hit me instantly.

"You'll get used to it," Mal said, reading my thoughts. Together, we crawled on our stomachs to the edge of the roof, where we would be able to see at least some of the battlefield below.

I peeked my head over slowly, and instantly sucked in a breath.

Our soldiers were ready. Every movement of a fae's weapon brought down one deadling, if not two.

In comparison to the skilled fighters, the deadlings were slow and unorganized. I scanned the battlefield, looking for a single sign of a fallen fae.

When I saw none, I took a deep breath and returned to the safety behind the ledge.

"See?" Malachi breathed, doing the same. "There's nothing to worry about. Serefin and the others have this under control. They could defeat an entire army of deadlings in their sleep."

"Really?" I asked. "And what happens after the deadlings? An army of witches?"

I couldn't shake the feeling that this was too easy. We knew they were coming. We had prepared for weeks. We called out to the surrounding kingdoms, and nearly all of our allies had come to help.

Luck never stayed by my side this much.

Another boom of a cannon shook the castle beneath us. Closer this time.

"Tessa would be freaking out if she were here," I breathed. I felt Malachi's attention snap to me. "In a weird, terrible way, I'm glad she doesn't have to deal with this. I just hope she's found peace."

Pain shot through my chest, but I quickly brushed it aside. This wasn't the time for pain. This was the time for focus.

"This world is no place for the innocent," he said. His words were so quiet at first, I thought I had imagined them.

But when I looked over to meet his eyes, I saw a face of so much sorrow, I could nearly feel the grief.

We had both been hurt. We had both been betrayed. We had both fought to survive until our fists bled, our hearts ripped.

This world was not kind. This world would chew you up and swallow you whole.

The shouting from the battlefield increased. By the sounds of it, the deadlings were beginning to die out. Next would be whatever army the Paragon had pulled together.

And they would not be as easy to defeat.

I leaned my head against the stone ledge behind me and closed my eyes. *Breathe, Jade. Breathe.* Malachi was right. This army would have no problem defeating any enemy of ours. We were large and experienced. We had numbers. We had the advantage.

"Are you afraid?" Malachi asked, snapping me from my thoughts.

"Yes," I answered. "But...it's a good kind of fear."

"A good kind?"

"It's...it's the kind of fear that makes you want to survive. That makes you want to keep living. I don't want to die, Mal. Not anymore."

He reached over and grabbed my hand, squeezing tight. "Nothing scares me more than losing you," he whispered.

Malachi's free hand found my cheek, and he slowly leaned over to kiss me.

My heart swelled as his mouth moved against mine. I could practically feel the goodbye in his lips.

But I kissed him back, anyway. I kissed him on that roof, holding onto him like he was all I had left in this world.

Another cannon struck the castle wall.

And the screams of battle began.

CHAPTER 34
Malachi

Every instinct in my body told me to fly down to that battlefield and pick up my sword.

But holding Jade in my arms caused me to stay.

"We should help them," she said. "If we use our power from here, they'll never know."

"They'll know you're here," I replied. "It'll be a dead giveaway."

"How?" she asked. "They have no clue what type of power I have. And they won't be able to tell where it was coming from."

"They'll storm the castle to find you," I replied. "Using our power is a last resort, Jade. The less they know about our power and what we have, the better."

She nodded, drinking in every one of my words.

Jade was a fighter. She had rough edges. She had grit and determination and strength.

I knew all of this, yet I was still not ready to send her to war.

"This entire war is happening because they want you, Jade," I explained again. "And I'm not letting them take you."

Her soft hands found my face in the setting sun. "I know you won't."

We stayed there for what felt like hours, although it couldn't have been more than a few minutes. War had that effect.

Scream after scream, we sat on the roof of the castle, praying to the saints that the screams were from our enemies.

A few stray arrows landed on the roof ahead of us, but it was nothing to be concerned about. Nobody knew we were here. They certainly wouldn't expect us to be hiding on the roof.

"Do you think Esther is still alive?" Jade asked.

My fists instinctively tightened. Esther could die on that battlefield, I didn't care.

It wasn't just that she had betrayed me. She was going to hurt Jade, too.

Jade might trust her again after what she did, but Esther wouldn't be receiving that same trust from me.

Never again.

"If she's on that battlefield," I answered, "I hope she's dead already."

Jade flipped over and began peeking her head over the wall, peering onto the battlefield. I didn't stop her from looking. Instead, I did the same.

Deadlings covered most of the ground. I couldn't even see the green grass anymore. Bodies and blood together covered the dark green that used to cover it.

But the deadlings were no longer the issue.

Carlyle had been right. Thousands of soldiers now

clashed with our own, metal clashing metal as they pushed onward.

Our soldiers were standing strong. The walls of the castle still went untouched. Not a single enemy fighter got past our defenses.

But men spread out as far as my eyes could see. This battle was only beginning.

Jade saw it, too. She saw the forest around us infiltrated with enemy soldiers. Some fae. Some, by the lack of wings, appeared to be witches. But they all fought with weapons.

There was no sign of the Paragon yet. No sign of Silas.

Something deep in my bones told me there would be a sign soon. Very soon.

My eyes landed on Serefin, who was standing back-to-back with Eli. Together, they defended the front gates of the castle. My other brothers were close by doing the same.

Emotion stung my chest. Not long ago, I had thought of my brothers as heartless, idiot men who would rather sit around the castle doing nothing than fight for this kingdom.

Saints, was I wrong.

"I should go down there," I mumbled.

Jade's eyes snapped to mine. "What?" she hissed. "No!"

"I'm their king, Jade. I should be down there fighting side by side with them. Not hiding on the roof like a coward."

"And what about me? How is that any different from what you've asked me precisely not to do?"

I opened my mouth to reply, but shut it again. Jade was right. If I went down onto that battlefield, there was nothing stopping Jade from doing the exact same.

And something told me it wouldn't take her long.

"Even if you could control your power," I explained, "it

would be too dangerous. You could easily take out one of our men."

"I'll be careful, Mal. You know I will."

"They'll overpower you. If someone came at you with a sword, you would be overtaken."

She shook her head. Saints, I hated how defiant she was. But at the same time, I loved her even more because of it.

"If you really want to help, you can do it from the safety of this roof. Do you understand?"

"But I–"

"I swear to the Saints, Jade Weyland, if I see you on that battlefield, I will lock you in the dungeons myself."

That seemed to shut her up.

"Fine," she said. "But be careful out there, Mal."

She threw her body at mine, pressing one last kiss onto my lips before pulling away.

I wanted more time with her. I wanted a lifetime of her mouth against mine.

This was the only way.

"Stay safe," I mumbled to her. I stood from the roof and dove to fight with my kingdom.

I landed fast and hard on the ground just inside the gate. The sun had fully set, giving me the cover of darkness as I prepared for battle. The ground shook beneath me and my power practically begged to be let loose. I unsheathed my sword and tucked my wings tightly behind my back.

There was no turning back now.

I leaped to the top of the wall, looking at the crowd of chaos below me. There were dozens of casualties, but I avoided looking at their faces.

We would mourn the dead later.

Now, we had to protect the living.

I spotted my brothers first. They were fully capable of taking care of themselves, but I leapt to the ground next to them anyway. Fae I didn't recognize fought against us, but they were no match.

Our steel cut deeper.

Our soldiers fought harder.

My brothers pushed forward on my left. I stepped right, slicing my sword through the torso of a young male.

My body buzzed with energy. The battlefield felt familiar in a way I could never explain. And I did not feel threatened.

My body moved without my permission. I sliced at anyone who came toward me, cutting down each enemy with ease. My power rumbled in my blood but I kept it at bay. Although my wings had been a dead giveaway as to who was fighting on this battlefield, my power would certainly put a target on my back.

I had enough to fight for.

Eli caught my attention. He looked ten years older now, wielding his sword with blood already splattered across the side of his face. He didn't look like a scared, inexperienced boy.

Eli fought like a warrior next to our brothers. With a battle cry, he grabbed his sword with both hands and brought it down–hard–against an approaching fae.

The body landed with a satisfied thud.

He didn't stop there. I watched as he ran forward, toward the forest, with a determination that others followed.

Back to reality.

I dodged a sword to my right, and my blade made contact

with flesh as I swiped my weapon in front of my body. Another fae down.

Another body.

I stepped on top of the corpse and cut down another.

And another.

Saints. These soldiers must have been inexperienced in battle. I caught the look of a few terrified faces just before death greeted them.

This was no place for the weak.

"Malachi!" Ser's voice pulled my attention to the left. "Malachi, get out of here!"

"I'm not leaving, Ser!" I yelled as I sliced the head off another attacker. "This is my kingdom. I'm fighting!"

Serefin sliced his way toward me, cutting down two more fae and stepping over their bleeding bodies. "Then I'm not letting you leave my sight," he mumbled.

Together, we pushed forward, leading the army in battle as we pushed the troops further and further from the front gate of the castle.

CHAPTER 35

Jade

My legs shook as I ran, down and down that stupid spiral staircase. I wasn't planning on leaving the roof. I didn't plan on disobeying Malachi's direct orders. But watching him leap over that wall and into battle...

No. I wouldn't stand by and watch as my life was ripped from me again.

The front doors would still be bolted closed. There was no way I was getting out of there. I had to think.

How else could I make it out of this damned castle?

I ran down the hallway that Mal had led me through not even an hour before.

There was a servant's exit. I had heard him speak of it before, the servants would never use the front doors to the castle.

That would be my way out.

I ran, looking for any door that looked short or hidden. Those doors would be the ones to lead me outside.

And before I knew it, I was pushing a small wooden door open to the outside.

I was on the side of the castle now, not anywhere near the front.

But I could still feel the tension in the air. The smell of death was even stronger now. And it would only get stronger.

Darkness hid me in its comforting shadows as I kept one hand on the stone castle wall, letting it lead me to the front.

I heard the screams first. The towering wall stopped me from viewing any of the fighting, but from what I saw on the roof, I was close.

I just had to get over that damned wall.

I took a deep breath and bolted, closing the distance from the castle to the wall that now separated me from the battle.

Power pulled on my chest. I knew I could wield it if necessary. I only hoped I wouldn't have to.

The knife Malachi had given me ages ago fit firmly in my hand. My palm was sweating, but not from nerves.

No. I was prepared for battle.

Malachi might not have thought so, but I sure did.

A flicker of light caught my attention ahead of me.

There were other entrances to the kingdom. I knew there were.

I crept forward, careful to stay as silent as possible in the throes of screams and screeches of metal clashing.

It was an opening. A small, hidden opening in the massive stone walls.

Saints.

I knelt on all fours, my knees and palms pressing against the cool, damp night ground. When I caught a glimpse of what was waiting for me on the other side of that hole...

My blood froze in my veins.

The first thing I noticed was the pile of deadlings that accumulated near the wall.

And the smell that came with them.

The soldiers had pushed away from the wall, though. There wasn't a single soldier within fifty feet of the wall now. They were pushing back.

That was good.

Right?

I knelt through the small opening in the wall.

This was it. There was no going back now.

I squinted against the darkness, trying to identify anyone familiar. A mixture of wings and weapons clashed ahead of me, but everything was too dark. Too far.

I couldn't see a single damn thing.

"I've been waiting for you," a male voice made me jump. I tightened my grip on my weapon and stood from my crouching position.

A large, hooded male stood before me. I couldn't see his face under the black shadows.

"Jade Weyland," he spoke. "You're coming with me."

"Who are you?" I asked. I tried to slice my weapon toward him, but he easily caught my wrists.

A low, blood-curdling laugh escaped him. Accompanied with the screams of battle. "My name is Silas," he said. My legs shook beneath me. "And you have something I want."

I screamed as loudly as I could before Silas lifted me off the ground.

CHAPTER 36
Malachi

Serefin and I heard her at the same time.

"Is that Jade?" he asked me in the midst of battle. Our enemies had thinned out in forces, but they were still coming.

Saints. I didn't even have to think about it. Yes, that was Jade.

I dropped another fae male to his knees before spinning around, looking for her in the darkness.

But chaos erupted around us, more with every second. I couldn't see past the spraying of blood and wings.

I couldn't hear past the battle cries of my men.

Dammit, Jade.

As our forces moved forward, pressing the enemy back, Ser and I moved toward the castle.

Toward Jade's scream.

She was okay. She had to be okay. I couldn't live with another possibility.

Ser and I trampled over dead bodies as we got closer and

closer to the castle wall. She was nearby. I could feel it, I could feel my power deep inside recognizing hers.

A cool blade pressed against the back of my neck. "Kneel," a voice I recognized demanded.

Every one of my senses lit a fire. I could end them with a single thought.

But where would that leave Jade?

Would Serefin die, too?

"Just do it, Mal," Serefin demanded. He already knelt next to me, a similar blade on his own person.

So I knelt.

"The mighty Prince of Shadows," the voice said. I wanted to vomit when I recognized just who was speaking...

Silas.

"Or is it *King of Shadows* now?"

"Where's Jade?" I asked. When I tried to turn my head, the blade on my neck pressed harder into my skin.

"Your wife is safe," Silas answered. "For now. I must say, I'm a bit disappointed. After everything I heard about her..."

Jade whimpered in the distance. She was maybe fifteen feet behind me.

"Let go of me!" she growled. A breath of relief came from me. She was alive. She was alive and fighting.

My power rumbled. I could end them. I had to.

But so could Jade. *Why hadn't she used her power to get away?*

I closed my eyes and focused on my senses. Silas stood behind my left shoulder, just far enough that I couldn't see his face.

Serefin was a few feet to my right, kneeling beside me.

And Jade was directly behind me. I assumed she had a soldier on each arm keeping her stable.

Five against three. *I liked those odds.*

"I just want to chat," Silas said. His boots crunched the forest floor as he stepped forward into view.

Just as hideous as I remembered.

"I'd rather not," I spat back. I let my power flare in his direction.

Silas fell to his knees before he could even get a good look at me. I sent a rush of power toward Jade, too, toward the guards that held her.

We had one advantage. They didn't know that Jade blocked my power. They had no idea how special she was.

I couldn't see her, but I heard her. Jade cried out as the soldiers let go of her. Serefin was next, but he was already fighting. The guard behind him still had a grip on his sword.

So I sent my own into his chest.

Jade ran toward me, and I caught her in my arms.

"Stay by me," I whispered. "Do everything I say."

I turned my attention back toward Silas, who still knelt on the forest floor, and to Serefin, who now had his sword aimed directly at Silas.

"Give me the order," Ser barked. "Say the words and he's dead."

Battle littered the air around us. I couldn't think straight. Couldn't breathe. My heart pounded again and again in my chest, faster than I ever thought possible.

"It's no use," I muttered. "Let's get out of here while we can."

Serefin hesitated for a moment. I knew he was registering the shock of what I had just said.

But I couldn't explain now. I couldn't explain it all.

Silas couldn't be killed.

At least, not in any way that I knew how.

Jade's power was on the verge of losing control. I felt it in my own body, rumbling and begging for release.

I sent another wave of power toward Silas, keeping him on the ground moaning in pain as the three of us began running toward the castle.

Not before Jade's father jumped out of hiding and brought his sword down on Silas.

CHAPTER 37
Jade

My blood froze as my father's weapon pierced Silas's flesh.

"Father!" I yelled. I ripped myself from Mal's grasp and ran toward him. His sword was still sticking out of Silas's back, but he wasn't moving.

Neither of them were.

"Father, what are you doing? Come on!" I yelled. "We have to get out of here!"

"I'm not leaving," he said. I felt Malachi's power rumble through the ground, aimed at Silas to keep him down.

"There's no time for this. If you stay here you'll die."

"You are my daughter!" he screamed. The chaos of battle seemed to fade in the distance. "I will not run while there are monsters like him trying to kill you!"

My body trembled with emotion I couldn't even understand. *Why was he doing this? Why now?*

Malachi yelled my name behind me, but I ignored him as I grabbed my father's arm and began pulling him with us.

Serefin yelped in pain. When I turned to see what was happening, he and Malachi were both on the ground.

Three hooded figures approached.

I knew exactly who they were from the chilling in my bones.

The Paragon.

They were here for me.

Not a single soldier stayed behind. Rewyth's entire army had pressed forward, focused on keeping the attackers away from the castle.

Yet somehow, these enemies snuck through. Fear pricked my senses as I remembered what I had learned about the Paragon. They were each *gifted*.

"Jade Weyland," a hooded figure said. Silas stood behind me. My father grabbed me by the shoulders and began backing up slowly. "I hear you are the alleged peacemaker. Is this true?"

I opened my mouth to speak but I froze. Malachi was still on the ground. One of these hooded men kept him there, I was sure of it.

"Jade is my daughter," my father yelled. "You will not take her!"

Silas shook his head as he stepped into view. "Your daughter seems to have a secret. If you are the peacemaker, we need to know. My people have been waiting on her arrival for centuries now. It is in everyone's best interest if she comes with us."

"Bullshit!" my father yelled.

The hooded figures stepped forward. Malachi tried to stand but failed. "It's honorable," the hooded figure started, "that you protect your daughter this way. I am interested to know, though, were you protecting her when you sent her to marry the Prince of Shadows? When you sold her off to the fae lands?"

I couldn't see my father's face. At that moment, I was glad. My father had suffered plenty the last few weeks.

"I am not the peacemaker," I finally declared. "There's been some mistake. You have the wrong person. I am only a human, and I never wanted any part of this!"

Silas eyed me closely, but eventually turned his attention to Mal and Serefin. "Let them up." Whichever hooded figure that kept them pinned to the ground relaxed. Malachi was on his feet in a second.

Silas held out his hand and said, "Not so fast. We want to handle this peacefully. If everyone cooperates, perhaps we can."

"You call this peaceful?" Mal spat. "Infiltrating my kingdom? I assume you call the other messengers you sent *peaceful* as well?"

"You would have never given up the girl otherwise."

"She is not a tool for some prophecy. And she is not going anywhere. She is my *wife*. You will *not* take her."

His words were strong, but I knew deep down we were at the end of this road. Desperation crept through my body. *They shouldn't die for me. They had done enough.*

"What do you want from me?" I asked Silas, pleading for any way out of this situation. "If I truly *were* the peacemaker, why would you need me? To kill me in some ritual? Sacrifice me for the greater good?"

"It is custom that to prove you truly are the peacemaker, you must pass the Trials of Glory," he answered.

Malachi and Serefin seemed to freeze.

"No," Mal muttered.

"It is the only way to–"

"NO!"

"The Trials of Glory? What is that?" I asked.

Before Silas could answer, a flash of black and silver wings crossed my vision. Malachi tackled Silas effortlessly, and Serefin pulled his own sword on one of the hooded men. My power flared, and I didn't stop it this time.

Desperation and adrenaline mixed together to help me wield my deadly gift. I threw my hands in the direction of the Paragon members, and light exploded around us.

CHAPTER 38
Malachi

aints save us...

Jade's magic erupted. I didn't have to look where she aimed it. I already knew. I felt exactly what her power wanted as if it were my own.

Silas stiffened beneath me. I jumped to my feet, releasing my grip on him and turned my attention toward Jade.

This was everything I had been trying to avoid. They had seen Jade's power with their own eyes.

Even worse.

One of the hooded figures now laid motionless on the ground. The smell of burnt flesh watered my eyes.

I stepped in front of Jade and her father, who was also staring at her in awe.

"Don't touch her," I demanded. "Let it go."

Silas stood up and approached the remaining two hooded men. "You know we don't have a choice, Malachi. The peace-maker comes with us."

"Mal," Jade whispered behind me. "You have to let me go."

Did I just hear that right?

"Nobody's going anywhere," I demanded.

"We've been waiting on her. She'll be safe with us until the trials," Silas announced.

"No! She's a human! The trials are not for her!"

"They are," Esther's voice interrupted. I turned to find her walking toward us, entirely unscathed.

"Esther," Silas announced. "What a surprise."

"How do you know my mother?" I asked him. He only smiled.

Anger stirred in my bones. Something wasn't right. Something–

Jade screamed.

I twisted to look at her, and found one of the surviving hooded fingers with a sword piercing her chest.

No.

A sound of pure terror escaped me. I snapped her attacker's neck before catching Jade's lifeless body.

"No!" I yelled. "You're okay, Jade. You're fine. Stay with me."

"Mal?" she whispered. Her voice already sounded weak. Too weak.

I looked at the amount of blood pouring from her chest. It was too much, too much blood.

Her father fell to his knees beside us.

"Help her!" I yelled. "Someone help!"

Jade's eyes flickered shut. I shook her shoulders, screaming her name. This wasn't it. This wasn't the end.

Jade would not die here.

"Malachi," Esther whispered.

"No! This is their fault! He did this!" I said, pointing to Silas.

"We meant her no harm, Malachi," he said in a gentle voice. "This is not what we intended."

"Did you know about this?" I asked Esther. "Did you know they would kill her?"

"I didn't know," Esther replied. "I swear it! I swear to the Saints! But they *will* let me save her life. If they want their peacemaker back, they'll let me do this."

Silas began speaking, but Esther cut him off.

"Jade is the peacemaker. I know you have your speculations still, but it's true. If Jade is dead, you will wait centuries more for the next. Help me save her life."

I could hardly breathe. Hardly think. The only thing I could do was hold Jade's body in my arms.

"You can save her?" I questioned.

Esther knelt beside me, grabbing hold of Jade's arm. "My time here is over, son. Let me do this one last thing."

Esther began chanting in a language I didn't recognize. Her eyes closed, but she didn't let go of Jade.

Jade's father screamed somewhere behind me.

The remaining Paragon members watched, entirely helpless, as Esther chanted and chanted.

"What are you doing?" I asked. But my questions fell void. Esther had gone somewhere else. Her eyes moved in wild motions beneath her eyelids as the chanting grew louder and louder.

When I thought she couldn't get any louder, she fell to the ground.

Unconscious.

"Esther!" I yelled. Serefin crawled over to her, shaking her shoulders.

"Wake up!" he yelled at her. "Wake up, Esther!"

Jade twitched in my arms.

Jade.

Be okay. Be alive.

"Saints," I muttered. Her body moved once more. "Jade! Can you hear me?"

I shook her lightly. Her wound still poured blood.

And then she coughed.

"She's alive!" I yelled. "She's moving! Serefin, help me over here!"

Serefin left Esther on the forest floor and knelt on the other side of Jade.

Silas spoke next. "I'll heal your wife right now if you agree to the trials."

Emotions flooded my body. I didn't want to fight anymore. I didn't want any of this.

Jade would not survive the trials. They were not created for humans.

But as her body twitched back to life, blood began pouring even faster from her wound.

She had minutes left.

"Let me come with her," I begged. "At the very least, let me help her. She will be the one completing the trials, but she will not be dragged into the mountains alone."

Silas considered my words. Jade moved again in my arms and my heart dropped as she began opening her eyes.

"You have yourself a deal, King of Shadows."

The last hooded figure approached Jade. I didn't stop him as he held a hand an inch above Jade's open wound.

I watched as tendrils of light escaped his hand.

And began closing Jade's open wound.

"Your wife will live," the healer announced with a cold tone.

I took a breath and leaned down, pressing my forehead to hers. She didn't deserve this. She didn't deserve any of this.

And she certainly did not deserve what would be coming.

"We will see you and your wife at the Trials of Glory."

Printed in the USA
CPSIA information can be obtained
at www.ICGtesting.com
LVHW040841251023
761974LV00052B/1028